1

Published by Father and Sons Games, ISBN: 9781790304226

2137 E Cassidy Way, Eagle Mountain, UT, USA 84005
TheHerosTale.com

This is a work of fiction. Any similarity between the characters and situations within its pages and places or persons, living or dead, is unintentional and co-incidental.

Cover by Abagail Crangle, interior illustrations by Mark Hansen

A Tale of Heroes
Book One

Of Children
and Dragons

By Mark Hansen

Dedicated To:

Jodi, for loving me all these years, and putting up with me writing at crazy hours and fretting over the blog's traffic.

Brendon, for being such a great Narrator, and inspiring and developing the original game (The Hero's Tale).

Jacob, for being so excited about learning and writing, and about our stories.

Foreward

What you're reading is an experiment.

In January of 2018, as the publication of "The Hero's Tale", our fantasy role-playing game rule book (now available at TheHerosTale.com) became more and more of a possibility, even a reality, my sons and I got very excited abut storytelling and writing. So much so, that I decided to take some of the initial characters in our game's sample adventure, use its world as a setting, and begin a fiction blog.

To me, the thought of writing a full novel had always been daunting and overwhelming. How would I ever find the time to write 50-60,000 words? However, I could easily commit to writing two scenes a week. That's not much, right? I started by outlining about the first month of the story, then dove in.

It was a very different way of writing, and of publishing, a story. It required a different structure, a different flow, and a different work strategy.

- Each blog post, a "scene", would be short. At first, I set those numbers at between 300 and 750 words as a guide.

Later, I would adjust that target to between 500 and 900. I think that if you go too much longer, you won't capture a blog audience. If its much shorter, you won't be able to do much in search, and the scenes just don't develop.

- I would post two times a week.
- Each scene would be written from an omniscient point of view, but focused on the perspective of a different one of the main characters.

Now, as the year comes to an end, I have completed the first two main story arcs. I have plans and outlined scenes well into the next one, and I don't foresee an end. I'm envisioning this as an ongoing tale, with characters coming and going, like a soap opera or a serial comic, all set in the fictional fantasy world of the game, known as Wynne.

This is not a normal approach to writing a story. It doesn't allow a lot of room for revisions, and the structure is not like the common "Chapter in a Book" kind of flow.

Also, this book is a bit of documentation of my own growth in the 12 months I was writing it. A lot of the characters dealt with things I was dealing with, and my own writing (and illustration) skills improved over the year. I offer that partly as an excuse, and partly as a way of sharing my own experiences.

...But, overall, I'm pleased with it so far. I hope after reading this, you'll continue to follow the story on the web (at theherostale.blogspot.com), and continue to follow the characters!

- Mark Hansen, December, 2018

Table of Contents

Story Two ~ The Kids Aren't Alright ~ p 129

Part Four ~ Splitting ~ p 131

Part Five ~ Separation ~ p 155

Part Six ~ Distance ~ p 179

Part Seven ~ Reunion ~ p 213

Interlude ~ p 255

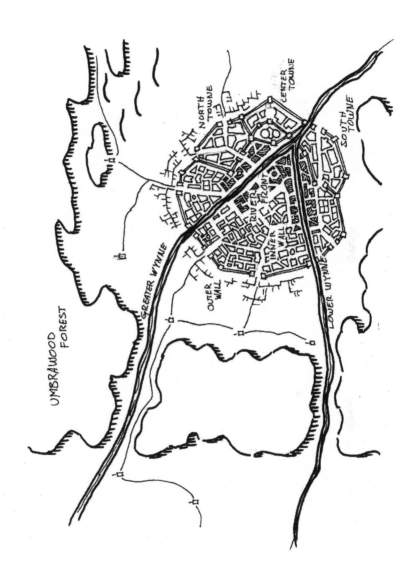

UMBRAWOOD FOREST

GREATER WYNNE

NORTH TOWNE

CENTER TOWNE

SOUTH TOWNE

RIVER FRONT

INNER WALL

OUTER WALL

LOWER WYNNE

Story One

Getting It All Together

Part One

Introductions

1
Rain, Rain, Go Away
DeFrantis

The late spring rain fell steady, straight down in the windless night. DeFrantis pulled her cloak hood down, trying to cover more of her face. The stones of the road were slick, and made it difficult to splash through the streets. At least the rains would wash off the mud and dung that had gathered since the last time a storm fell. In the InnerWall section of the city of Twynne Rivers, the buildings were packed in close, and when the rains came, the streets between them flowed freely. Partly because of that, and the time of night, the streets were empty.

Through the dim light of a nearby window, she found an inn with an overhanging second story and dashed through the pour to huddle underneath it. She was good at finding the shadows, and shrinking into them. She was human, but her youth and frail stature made her look almost elvish in the dark.

Her stomach grumbled. Yes, she was hungry, and that only reminded her that the other kids waiting in their hovel in the abandoned chapel beyond the city wall were hungry, too. It was true they'd been out begging, as usual, but the rains had been steady for two days, so there hadn't been many people out for them to bother. That meant that it was time to steal.

She could have done that in the OuterWall, of course. That would have even been easier to do, but, honestly, they were all tired of gruel and scraps. So, they convinced her to take the risk and hop the wall into the city proper. She'd done it many times, but this time, the wet rocks had been a bit more slippery than usual.

She moved along the side of the building toward what looked like the back. As she came to a window, she crouched under it, then rose up to a corner and peeked in. The interior was well lit with candles and lanterns, shining a warmth and friendliness in sharp contrast to the chilly wet of the rain. There were a half dozen patrons of the inn at various tables, eating heartily. The tables were sturdy, but worn. The room was sparsely decorated with a few ragged hangings. Up above were rafters, stained with years of soot from the fireplace, the candles, and smoking pipes of the patrons. She looked deeper in and saw the bar area with the innkeeper and his wife busily cleaning and serving the tables. She saw them smiling at each other, pleased for a busy night.

These people don't have much, either! What am I supposed to do? She turned away and hunched against the wall, drawing in her cloak for warmth. *I hate this!* She thought, *but the others are counting on me.*

The rain didn't care. Their hunger didn't care. She looked past some barrels down the dark, empty street. With a deep sigh, she moved.

2
Lights On The River
Granthurg

The early part of the spring had brought average rainfall. It might have even been a little dry this year. So two days of steady rain, while not strange, was still a little unexpected. It had raised the Wynne River up a bit past its normal levels. Not yet high enough to flood, but high enough to make the waters flow more swiftly. The Wynne was fairly deep and wide in the eastern parts, so there wasn't much worry of rapids or difficulty in maneuvering. Granthurg thought about this as he took his turn steering the long barge toward Twynne Rivers. Since they were on a downriver run, their two-man crew didn't even have to use their nature powers to drive the barges, like they typically would when going upstream.

He was easily eight feet tall, with thick, muscular shoulders and a bit of a belly, all well hidden under a heavy shirt. He stood on a raised platform on the stern of the barge, with a tight tarp stretched above his head to drip off the rain. It didn't give him a lot of headroom. The loads they were transporting were stacked and tied down on the barge deck before him, also covered.

Granthurg was one of the many giants that worked the river between his home in the western mountains and the cities of Twynne Rivers and PortsTown. They drove barges, some long, others smaller, up and down, driving trade with the villages along the way. The barge he drove was not the largest he'd ever seen, but he was happy to be on the crew.

At his left was another giant, asleep under a blanket. This was the barge owner and captain, Rinkmorr. He was larger, older, and more experienced that Granthurg, and had the natural powers

over water necessary to drive the loaded barge, against the current, back up to their home at the foot of the mountains. Granthurg hadn't learned those skills, yet. He was there to load, unload, and defend. Sometimes, when they went downstream, he was allowed to steer, as he was doing.

Even at night, there wasn't much to steering. He pretty much just had to keep the barge from running aground on the banks. There were two stones mounted on the front of the barge, magically shining light onto the waters before him, and allowing him to see if he got too close. These were the so-called oculi creatori - "the eyes of the Creator", gems that had been purified and enchanted by the Twynne Rivers wizard's guild. Most of the barges had them, even though they were expensive to acquire.

He squinted as he looked out over the dark, past the barge, past the light of the oculi, and into the rain. He thought he saw a glimmer of light up ahead along the river.

That's odd. We're not supposed to get to Twynne Rivers until later tomorrow. He looked closer, *and I don't remember a village on the way.*

He looked again. He definitely saw them, off to the right. They weren't in the configuration of a barge's oculi, and anything that far off to the side would have to be way too close to the banks, if not actually on the shore.

He looked on the floor behind him and saw his hammer. It was sitting there on the deck, as he had left it, ready for him to grab and swing if it was necessary. It was large, a two-handed weapon, and well-crafted. Its steel was ornately shaped, but hard and sturdy in combat.

He looked forward again. The lights were gone.

That's not good. His eyes scanned the dark ahead of him, hoping he would find the lights. *That's not good at all.* With one hand still gripping the rudder, he reached for the hammer.

He would be ready.

3
Up To My Tower
Thissraelle

I know it's not the tallest tower in Twynne Rivers, She thought, sliding her feet onto each step on the circular stairway, *but it might as well be.*

Usually, she would just float herself up to the small study at the top. She had the ability to use the power. It was a lot easier than climbing, and it was good practice. Tonight, however, she wanted to save her powers, and her will. Actually, it wasn't even the tallest tower in the guild hall. It was, however, her tower. She was Thissraelle, and her father was the Guildmaster of the Twynne Rivers Wizards' Guild. When she was very young, he had given her the room at the top as a place to study magic. He made it so it belonged entirely to her. But he also made it so she belonged to it.

She paused on the stairs as she passed a window. For a moment she caught her reflection in the glass, in spite of the rain splattering on the pane. Her face was thin and delicate, with a dainty, if sharp chin, and a small slope for a nose. Her father had often told her that she was beautiful, as all high elves were. Her gaze shifted out the window, over the city. She could see many lights glowing in the CenterTown below, even though the rainwater on the glass distorted her view. She knew well the bright oculus lights of the streets below. She leaned into the window well and swung the pane open, letting the cool air and a bit of the rain waft in onto her face and blow her thin long white hair.

Directly in front of her, and towering above, were the three bell towers of the Cathedral of The Church of Three Lights. A distance beyond that, and off to her left, she could see the palace, then the wall separating the luxurious CenterTown from the rough and tumble of the RiverFront, and the merchants in the NorthTowne. There were some lights in the streets there as well.

Beyond that lay the InnerWall, where the commoners lived, worked, and fought. Outside the city wall, there was only darkness. In the sun, during the day, she could see the mosaic made by the shanty roofs in the OuterWall. Here, at night, in the rain, there was only black beyond.

She had often wondered what life was like outside of CenterTown. Her father had told her frightening stories of the crime, poverty, and carnage that ruled beyond the wall. At first, she had listened, wide-eyed and terrified, but as she grew older, she began to wonder. If all of these stories were true, how could the city live? How would shops sell, and inns be kept? If all was chaos, how could the city go on?

And what would I find in the forests and mountains beyond Twynne Rivers? She had often wanted to see the world, and she wanted to start with a journey to Emberfire, the city of her people, the high elves. She had lived her entire life here in the center of Twynne Rivers, with the humans, and the only other high elves she knew were her mother and father.

...Until now!

With a secretive smile, she closed the window and continued up the stairs.

4
River Pirates
Granthurg

Granthurg stepped forward, to the edge of the platform, and squinted out into the dark rain. The oculus lamps shone, but revealed nothing but river and more rain.

What were those lights? They looked like they were gleaming from the shore... He ducked under the edge of the tarp and hopped off the platform. Instantly, he felt the chill of the rain falling on his face and bald head, and running onto his shoulders, soaking his shirt. He hefted his hammer and strode toward the bow of the boat. Maybe he could see better from there.

As he took the last steps to the bow, to stand next to the lights, he strained to see beyond the glow of the oculi. All he could hear was the torrential rain falling around him, on him.

He shrugged and shook off the wet as much as he could and turned around, to return to the steering at the stern.

Halfway back, along the side of the barge, he saw two men climbing over the railing from a small boat now alongside the barge. One jumped onto the walkway between the railing and the tarped cargo and drew a shortsword. He shouted and rushed toward Granthurg.

The giant's instinct was to defend himself, so he hefted the handle of his hammer between his two hands and used it to block the initial slashes of the sword. His attacker was significantly shorter than Granthurg, by at least a head and a half, and wearing a dark cloak. Behind him, another one stood, in an attacking posture, but unable to reach around past his cohort.

Granthurg continued blocking, and began pressing forward. He shifted his left hand, near the head of the hammer, then, after a block, lunged forward and used his leverage to swing the massive hammer in a side sweeping counter-attack. The boarder saw it coming and jumped back, but lost his footing on the rain-soaked deck and fell backward.

As he rolled over and struggled to stand, Granthurg raised the hammer up above his shoulder and swung down, narrowly missing the wriggling man's legs and cracking the planks of the deck.

Both men scrambled toward the stern, slipping on the wood.

Granthurg suddenly realized his friend and boss was there, sleeping. "RINKMORR!" he shouted, and hoped he could wake him before the river pirates got to him. He lunged forward, taking huge strides, and threw himself at the men. His hammer clattered to the deck as he wrapped his bulky arms around the nearest man's torso. They collapsed with a crash, and the impact of Granthurg's huge body swayed the boat back and forth.

"RINKMORR!" He called again, "GET UP! GET UP!"

5
Of Course!
Granthurg

The barge deck heaved up and down, and the rain made it slippery and hard to stand steady. The forward pirate grabbed the railing, trying to hold his balance. Granthurg punched the downed man under him, hitting him twice. The barge stabilized a bit, as did the pirate, and Granthurg lifted up to see him lunge. A sharp, cold pain stabbed into the giant's shoulder and he lost his balance, falling backward. He smashed onto the deck and the cargo crates, and struggled against the assault, knocking bags and barrels loose.

He looked up into the angry determined face of his assailant as the pirate pulled back on his sword and raised it for a second strike. Even though the man was smaller, he was positioned so as to make it difficult for Granthurg to move. He lifted his arms to shield himself, in spite of the pain.

At that moment, a deep splash of slimy river water rushed over him, down his throat, in his nose, and washed him further down the length of the barge. He rolled over as the water flowed past him, and coughed and gagged, gasping for breath. Finally, as his lungs and his head cleared, he knelt and looked up. Down the walkway, he saw Rinkmorr standing with his hands still forming the follow-through of a watershaping spell. The rest of the riverwater flowed off the barge, and Granthurg saw that the two pirates had been washed off with it.

Suddenly the awareness of the pain in his shoulder returned. He winced as he stood. The clean rain was gradually rinsing off the muddy river water, as well as the blood flowing from his wound. He grabbed the railing for balance, and raised his gaze to his friend.

"I could have handled them."

"Yeah. Of course." His boss smiled, with more than a hint of sarcasm. "I'll bet you could've."

6
The Problem With Chickens
DeFrantis

DeFrantis slipped under the window and continued creeping along the street to the back of the inn. As she went, she began to smell the aromas of cooking meats and stews wafting through another open window. It made her empty stomach beg. This was not the distraction she needed. She kept moving.

Soon the building ended and with it, the overhang. The wall she was leaning on changed to a fence. On the other side of it, she could hear a pig grunting. The smells had also changed. As she continued, the fence turned a corner, and the street branched to the right into an alleyway behind the inn. The rainwater flowed out of the alley and into the street. She hurried across and into the alley, with the splashes rushing over her feet.

Feeling along in the rain and the darkness, she found a gate. She tried it, and it was locked. She looked to the top of the fence, leapt up and grabbed for it. One of her hands slipped, and she shifted and reached again. She swung her body side to side, then pulled herself up and over. She landed, feet-first, in a pile of straw. Her footing slipped in the wet straw and she fell back against the fence.

A light shone into the stockyard from an open door in the back of the inn. She could hear someone inside along with clanging pots. That must be the kitchen. To her right was a lower fence and through its sparse slats, she thought she could make out a pig. Further away, on the left was a chicken coop. Most of the chickens were huddling inside, but a few were pecking around the straw, dung, and mud under an overhanging roof of the coop.

She leaned forward, crouching on her heels and began creeping toward one of the chickens.

"C'mere!" she hissed, trying to both whisper and be a bit louder than the rain. She tried making clucking noises. "Get over here!"

28

She moved forward, reaching for the chicken. It stood and stared at her as she got closer. She set herself for the spring, and threw herself at the chicken. It dodged away in a flurry of flapping and she landed in the muck.

The foul smell hit her immediately and she pulled herself up to her hands and knees. The clucking of the chickens sounded more like laughter to her. She scrambled to her feet and lunged at the nearest one, hissing, "You hold still!" She grabbed the chicken and stood with a surprised expression and questionable balance. She raised her eyes to look up at the angry innkeeper standing in the light of the doorway.

7
In a Bit of Trouble
DeFrantis

"You leave my chickens be!" The innkeeper grabbed a shovel leaning by the side of the door and stepped toward DeFrantis.

"Wait, wait..." she said, "I don't mean any harm! I just--" She began backing away, toward the fence.

"No harm would be not trying to steal my chickens!" He shouted, swinging the shovel before him. She dropped the chicken and jumped back, losing her balance. She went down with a splat in the mud and straw. Through the rain in her eyes, she could see him lifting the tool to swing at her again.

She lifted her hands, palms up, and willed herself to be hidden. The shadows all around her swelled up and swirled over her, enveloping her in darkness. She willed it outward, to cover the stockyard.

She heard the innkeeper gasp. "Wizardry!" Then she heard a crash. "I can't see you, but I can still hit you!"

She rolled to her side, then up to her feet. As quickly as she could with the slippery ground, she struggled to get to the back fence. When she reached it, she jumped up and tried to grab on and pull herself over. She slipped and fell with a splash.

"There you are!" He shouted through the rain, "I'll get you!"

She frantically curled up and tried to make herself as small as possible in the darkness of the shadow. She could hear him slogging through the mud toward her. He grunted as he swung the pitchfork, once, twice, then she heard only rain. *I'm so glad the others usually do this. I'm so bad at it!*

She cowered, breathing heavily, and trying to be silent. *I've got to get out. The shadow won't last forever. Is he gone?* With all the caution she could muster, she slid to her knees, then to her feet. She was near the fence, she was sure, so she reached behind her and felt it. She slowly turned in the dark.

She bent her knees slightly and jumped, reaching the top of the fence and grabbing on. She had swung herself up and hooked her leg over when she felt the sharp pain of impact on her head. It shot down through her whole body. She tensed, then fell, limp, into her own darkness.

8
Escape!
Thissraelle

After the final stair, Thissraelle entered the dark room at the top of the tower. The rain was making a steady rustle on the roof above. She waved her hand and three oculi began to shine, revealing her study table in the center of the room, cluttered with papers and books. Next to it was a huge bookshelf. She rushed to it, tossing herself to the floor at its base. From the bottom shelf she pulled a moderately sized wooden trunk. It clattered to the floor and she shushed it, then laughed at herself.

It's not like anyone can hear me up here anyway! Especially through the rain.

She took a small key from her pocket, undid the lock, then threw it open. For months, now, she had been stealing up the stairs and secreting things away in this trunk. She retrieved them, now. A heavy travelling cloak with a hood. Very finely made, with white and blue trim, it would be especially useful tonight in the downpour.

character
studies
Thirouelle
RWH
4/25/18

Earlier in the night, she had contemplated postponing her escape for the weather. *Escape? Is that the right word?* She thought about that for a minute, and looked around at the tower. She loved this place. It was her solace and her place of learning. It was also her cell, along with the guild hall and the CenterTown below, trapping her as securely as a prison.

But in the end, she had decided that she had to stick with her plan. That was when she had snuck away, after dinner, after her parents were preparing for bed. Rain or not, she had to escape. Really, the rain would help. The storm clouds would darken the cover the night would give.

She slung a pouch over her shoulder. It had a few changes of clothing, a small blanket, some coins and gems, and some bread and cheese she'd brought up earlier in the day. She swirled the cloak over her shoulder and clasped it under her chin.

She leapt to her feet and pulled the hood over her head. It was only a few quick steps to the door, and she was out on the small balcony, feeling the cool wet air on her face. She looked up into the rain and smiled.

She lifted her arms to welcome the clouds and willed herself up into the air. She spun through the rain out of sheer excitement, then flew away from the tower.

9
...Or Not An Escape
Thissraelle

As she rushed through the air, away from her tower room, the rain fell into her eyes. She pulled the hood lower and wiped the water away. When she looked again, she froze, then willed herself to stop only a few feet away from, could it be? Her tower? She glanced up at the roof. It was there on the roof that she had spent many nights learning about the stars. It was through that window that the morning light had shone on her magical studies.

Yes, it was her tower! She could see the light shining out through that same window! *But there's no balcony! What's this?*

She spun around and instantly recognized the view of the city. *I'm on the other side of the tower! How did I get here?*

She floated in the rain, confused, looking back and forth from the tower to the empty air over CenterTown.

I went that way, she mused, pointing past her room, then turning, *and came from that way...* She pointed the opposite direction. *I wonder...*

Slowly, then building speed, she floated away from the back side of the tower, out into darkness, and in a moment found herself floating before the balcony where she had stood just moments before. Its warm and familiar light looked odd from the outside. She floated forward. Light and understanding were also gathering in her mind. Understanding that troubled her.

My father! He's enchanted this tower! He knew someday I would try this. He knew I would want to leave. She hovered there, clenching her fists, frustration swelling inside her. *I really AM trapped. I really AM a prisoner!*

She threw her head back and screamed into the rain. She screamed again. Finally, in dejection, she drifted down onto the balcony, opened the door and stepped back inside. Her shoulders shook. Her eyes dripped more rain onto her cloak, and onto the floor.

10
If, At First, You Don't Succeed...
Thissraelle

I know my father loves me. I know he's just trying to protect me. She sat and cried without sobbing. *I want to leave! I want to live!*

She took off the dripping cloak, and the bag, and lay back on the floor, looking at the ornate ceiling like she had done thousands of times before. Her eyes traced the shadows of the intricate woodworking on the rafters. She let her thoughts drift off into mindlessness, needing to escape her frustration. Her eyes continued along the lines above, tracing the sculpting, the inlays, the frills.

With a deep sigh, she closed her eyes. She wasn't tired. She was looking for peace, and not finding it.

WAIT! She blinked, and her eyes narrowed. *If my father enchanted this tower, it would have had to have been done a long time ago. It would take a lot of will to maintain it that long.* Her heart raced and she sat up. She scanned the ceiling again.

He wouldn't use his own will for that power. He'd put it into an oculus, and hide that in the room! But where is it? She'd never paid much attention to the stones inlaid in the ceiling. They were just a part of the room's decor. She levitated up to the rafters and began looking more intently. As she found them, she touched them, felt them. They were all just cold gray stones of granite. That realization made her smile. Gray is the color most often associated with dimensional wizardry. *The kind of powers that could warp and fold space in around itself so that one couldn't leave,*

34

say, a room or tower?

Her hands touched each inlay in turn, and felt nothing but cold stone. She felt herself getting tired and knew that she couldn't keep flying much longer.

She felt a shiver. Was that something, or just from being out in the rain? She moved her hand back to the stone she had been touching. She felt it again, stronger, this time, as she focused on it. *That's it! That's it!* She could definitely feel the familiar latent power emanating from it.

I've felt that all these years, and just hadn't realized it.

She wasn't sure what do do with it, though. She grabbed at it with her fingernails, but wasn't strong enough to pry it free.

This is dimensional wizardry, isn't it? My father taught me some, so I can play in that game, too! She hesitated, uncertain. *I can't send it away, or shatter it. He is way more powerful than I am. What if I use my own power to twist reality around it? I can make a dimensional warp around its own dimensional warp, and shrink it down. Then I'll be outside of its reach, at least for a few minutes!*

She looked down at the study below her. *My will is getting weak. I'll need more strength! Where can I find more?* She saw the table, chairs, books, shelves, all lit up by the glowing oculi.

The oculi! She swept to the floor and put on the bag and the cloak again. She rushed over to the nearest oculus on the wall and reached up to surround it with her hands. Focusing on it, deeper, and deeper still, she stared into its glow.

A little at first, she felt its energy flowing into her hands, and arms. *Yes, more! I need more!* The lamp flickered, dimmed, then went out. She rushed to the second one, then the third.

Re-energized, she flew up again, and looked for the dimensional stone. It was difficult to find, now, in the dark, but she felt for it. She surrounded it with her will, and concentrated. Suddenly, she felt a nauseating wave of rippling reality sweep over her as it shrunk to converge on the stone. She blinked and backed away. *I hope that worked! I won't have much time!*

In a moment she had flown through the door and was lost, laughing, in the dark rain over the city.

11
Healing Nature
Granthurg

Rinkmorr lit a lantern and hung it up under the tarp. Its glow spread all over the steering platform, showing the rain dripping off the shelter and the darkness around them. Granthurg was standing at the edge of the platform, looking out over the river past the barge. Since the two pirates had been defeated, he had been scanning the slowly growing morning glow on the horizon looking for more. There had been none. The bleeding in his shoulder had stopped, but not the pain.

"Ok, let me look a that wound." Rinkmorr said, pulling a box up, and gesturing to Granthurg to sit. Granthurg turned and obeyed. Once he was seated, he pulled back his shirt from his shoulder.

Rinkmorr looked. "That's a deep hit."

"Yeah," Granthurg smiled, "It really wasn't very knife of him to do that."

36

The older giant narrowed his eyes and nudged the wounded shoulder, turning the smile to a wince. "Did that hurt?"

"No." Granthurg could see that Rinkmorr didn't believe him. "Well, not much anyway."

"This river's getting more and more dangerous. There was a time when I didn't have to hire extra muscle." He leaned over and felt the wound. Granthurg winced again.

Rinkmorr stood, closed his eyes, and breathed deep, focusing his concentration. Granthurg saw a brief grimace on his face, as if he was feeling the pain, too. Then, he felt the energy of life swell up in them both, drawn from the waters, the land, and the trees. Granthurg also took a breath, almost involuntarily, and held it in, savoring the feeling as the hurting faded.

Then the sensations also drained from him, back into the river, and he let out the breath. His shoulder was healed. As the two giants opened their eyes, Rinkmorr offered his hand, then pulled Granthurg up.

"Someday, you'll have to teach me how to do that," Granthurg smiled. Then, he stepped to the steering rudder at the stern of the platform.

Rinkmorr lay back down on the blankets padding the deck. "It'll be dawn soon, and then we'll be in Twynne Rivers. I'm gonna get some sleep."

It wasn't long before the rain on the tarp was punctuated by his snoring. Granthurg adjusted his shirt and watched out over the barge across the night.

Prayers in the Dark
Antonerri

Antonneri lay on the cold stone floor of the holding cell, the dark of doom swirling in the smoky air around him. He had been to places like this before, but always on the other side of the bars. A faint glow from a small table across the main room cast faint shadows around him. His muscles ached, his head ached. Even deeper, his heart ached. And through the ache was a core of confusion.

He rolled over and heaved himself up onto his knees and hands. His physical aches were the residue of blasts of light power he had received at the hands of a Sacerdotis Confessoris - The Priest Confessor of the Church of Three Lights. His deeper aches and confusion were also residual of the same blasts.

He had grown up in the shadow of the Church, serving as a young boy, longing for the day that he could join the Holy Guard as a soldier of The Creator. When he achieved that goal, it was the happiest day of his life. As a holy soldier, he was ready to defend the weak and serve the downtrodden.

His early duties were not so exciting, mostly protecting high priests and relics. He didn't mind, though. He was proud to wear the three lights on his chest.

He sat back on his heels, kneeling into a familiar position of prayer. *Please,* he began, *help me understand!*

Memories of a few short days ago filled his mind. He had been assigned with a corps of The Guard to protect a Count of the Twynne Rivers High Council as he traveled through the InnerWall area of the city, gathering taxes from his subjects. All went well for the first few stops, then they came upon a shopkeeper who couldn't pay.

Antonerri saw the image of the poor man's crying face as he begged for more time. The troop was ordered to "render justice" by beating him and seizing his property.

What did I do that was wrong? Please, help me see!

He saw the rage on the face of the Count as Antonerri refused to execute the order. Then he saw the other soldiers of the Guard, his colleagues, turn on him, beating him, binding him, and delivering him to the dungeon of the guard tower in the wall.

His pains intensified as he remembered The Priest Confessor's visit.

His own tears streamed down as he prayed. *I just want to know why! Am I not there to protect the weak? Why am I here?*

The acrid smoke in the room added to the burning in his eyes and the gloom covering his heart. He knew the smell. It reminded him of the times he had captured a thief or a heretic and brought them to a place like this. He had thought they deserved this treatment for their sins and their crimes. All those times he never dreamed he would be one of them.

With a creak, a door near him opened and a brighter glimmer of light slashed into the space, broken only by the metal bars that grew up from the floor in front of him to reach the ceiling.

The door parted further and two guards of the city's militia stepped in, dragging a body in a rain-soaked black cloak between them. In a spare hand, one of them carried a lantern that cast spinning shadows as it swung under his hand. They lurched past his cell. After fussing with the keys, they swung the door to the neighboring cell open, and dropped the other prisoner inside. One of the guards moved to the table and tossed a few more grains of incense into a small metal bowl smoldering there. The other clanged the cell door shut, then glared at Antonerri.

"Yeah, you'd best be praying!" He said in a raspy voice, then laughed as they both closed the main door behind them. Dark and sorrow closed around Antonerri again as he bowed his head.

Part Two

Connections

13
Thievery and Wizardry
DeFrantis

Her first deep breath of consciousness brought a fit of coughing and hacking. The thick air was tough to take in. DeFrantis rolled over onto her belly and tried to lift herself up on her hands and knees. The second sensation was a sharp, but steady pain in her head and neck. That dropped her back down with a moan. Next came the cold, from lying on a stone floor in dripping wet clothes.

She lay, slightly shivering, as her breathing steadied, and her eyes took in her surroundings. She saw the shadows of the bars of the cell holding her on the stone walls on the opposite side. She raised up on her elbow and squinted through the haze. She could make out the form of a door and a table, and another cell next to hers. She thought she could see a dim shape up against the far wall. Could it be... a person? She couldn't be sure. She sat up, slowly, this time, and brought her arms tight to her chest, to hug off the cold. Her cloak was drenched and only making her colder. She unbuckled it and let it fall back.

"Are you awake, now?"

She reflexively jumped and rolled to the corner of the wall where the shadows were darkest, and curled up to be as invisible in the dark as possible. The voice had been quiet, but it had startled her nonetheless.

"You are."

She passed her hand in front of her, and tried to will up the shadows around her, to hide her, but nothing happened. Confused, she tried again. Nothing. She tried controlling her breathing to make herself silent, and waited. But he didn't move, and said nothing else.

Finally, she spoke. "Who are you?"

"Another prisoner, like you. A heretic, apparently."

42

She began to feel another sensation, the pangs of deep hunger. "How long have I been here?" She wondered, out loud.

"Hours, maybe. Probably not more than a day. It's hard to tell down here."

"Where is that?" She began to creep toward her cloak.

She heard him sigh. "You're in a holding cell under one of the guard towers built into the InnerWall. You're here because you were arrested."

The scenes of the night played through her mind swiftly. In all her life, she had never been caught stealing. She didn't like it, and she knew she wasn't especially good at it, but she'd never been caught, either.

She heard him move, repositioning himself on the floor. He said, "What did you do?"

"I tried to steal some chickens."

He laughed. "A thief!"

"It's not like that!" She hissed, "There are kids that are hungry. They count on me!"

"Still..." He thought a minute. "I'm surprised they'd put a chicken thief here in the dungeon. Usually they'd just beat you and toss you back to the OuterWall. You must have done something particularly bad."

She bristled at that. "No, I didn't! I just tried to take--"

"Did you use magic?" Her silence was his answer. "I'll bet that's it."

"Magic isn't illegal. That wouldn't be right!"

"Do you think 'legal' matters down here? Do you think 'right' matters?" He laughed again, "Nothing matters down here."

Then more silence.

14
Smoke and Gloom
DeFrantis

I've got to keep trying! DeFrantis stood in the center of her dark stone cell and slowly extended her hands out in front of her. She closed her eyes and focused her mind on the part of the room just beyond her cell bars. She dug deep into herself and gathered her will, her strength.

Please, please! Just let me open a small portal! Let it work!

But she felt nothing.

There was no surge of power from within, no welling up of confidence or determination. Nothing to show her that there was any personal will inside to draw on. She was an empty dry well of... nothing but smoky darkness.

She leaned forward, pushing outward with her hands. "OPEN!" She commanded, pushing,"OPEN!"

She lost her balance and fell to her knees on the cold stone floor. The smoke filled her as she heaved her breathing. She coughed, hard.

Antonerri moved to the bars between their cells and stood, resting his arms on the crossbars. "Powers won't work here in the dungeons of the towers." He muttered. "I've tried."

"Why not? Why can't I do it?"

"It's not you, it's the incense they're burning. It's called mage's bane. It suppresses your mood and your will." She looked at him, confused. She glanced over at the smoldering bowl dimly lit on the table beyond the cells, then turned back to Antonneri. From this distance she could see him a little better than before. He was tall, and his shadowed face was hidden further by a few day's beard stubble. He was wearing a white tunic, with the three-starred emblem of the Church on his left shoulder. "If you've never breathed it before, it's probably affecting you more. That's probably why you haven't wanted your gruel." He gestured by her cell door, to the half-empty bowl.

She hadn't noticed it before. Suddenly, her empty aching stomach overtook her and she crawled over to it. It looked horrendous in the dark and smog, and there was no spoon. She picked it up and smelled it, then used her two fingers to scoop a little into her mouth.

It was bland, but not the worst thing she'd ever eaten. She took a second mouthful, then another.

She paused to ask, "So, will we ever leave? Will there be a tribunal?"

"Maybe." He leaned his head against the bars. "A Sacerdotis Confessoris - a confessor priest - will come in and read you your charges."

DeFrantis noticed a darker tone to his voice. "What happens then?" She asked, trying not to show her fear.

"That depends on how you answer them. If you confess your sins and beg for repentance and redemption, your punishment may be light, and your freedom quick." His tone was sharp, almost sarcastic. He turned and walked back into the darkness of his cell. She heard him sit down.

46

"Aren't you part of the Church? They should let you go! Your tunic has..." After a moment's hesitation, she ventured, in a hush, "I'm guessing that you haven't properly asked for forgiveness, yet, have you?"

He let out a sigh. "It would help if I understood my sins."

The sorrow in his voice weighed heavily on her like the dark gloom of the cell. She sat back with her gruel. *It must just be the incense, right?*

15
Wizards
Karendle

By noon, the rains had stopped in Twynne Rivers. As the afternoon grew, the sky was still overcast, but at least it wasn't crying like it had been for the last three days. The streets were still wet, even puddled, and sometimes still flowing.

People wasted no time getting back to business, slogging over the paving stones and occasionally the mud to get their burdens where they needed to go. Shops opened their windows and doors.

Karendle weaved her way between the people as she hurried past them. She wasn't tall, but she was stocky, with stout shoulders and long, thick hair braided behind her. Her face was round, with full cheeks below brown eyes.

She looked at the banners hanging above the doorways as she walked. *The Brown Boar Inn. There it is! Just like they said it would be.*

Knut
3/18/18
Karendle

She stepped up, opened the door, and passed inside. It took a minute for her eyes to adjust to the dimmer light. At the far end was a fireplace, and there were several strong wooden tables scattered around the floor. There weren't too many patrons yet, so she moved to one of the tables and sat down.

Her father had been a dwarven gem trader in the western mountains, and had returned from Twynne Rivers with a new human wife. They soon had a daughter, naming her Karendle, and as she grew up, she felt the differences between herself and the full blooded dwarves around her. She was taller, but not so strong, and often felt out of place. That was made worse by her desire to learn magic. Her mom knew a bit of the powers, and had tried to teach her, but it never seemed to click into place for her.

Finally, after coming of age, she determined to go to the great city and see if she could learn the powers directly from the elves there.

The plump and smiling innkeeper's wife interrupted her memories and asked in a loud, friendly tone, "What can I get for you?"

48

"Just a meal with some ale."

"Is chicken and bread good for you?"

"Sure."

Karendle had traveled down the river, and sought out the Wizard's guild. It hadn't been easy to find them, and they were none too happy to see her. They had one of their instructors humor her with a quick exam, then dismissed her as uninstructable. "You don't have the... the spark inside you. You'll never be a mage." The more she pressed them, the stronger their denials became. Finally, they had expelled her from their guild hall, and from CenterTown.

A few more patrons had begun to flow into the inn, as dinnertime drew closer. Some took seats at tables, others went back to the bar to talk to the innkeeper. The evening pubcrier stepped in, and everyone turned to listen as he rattled off his announcements and news. It was typical things, a pronouncement of taxes from the King, news of a band of wizards being arrested for attacking a shopkeeper on the RiverFront, and a Councilman decrying the attack and calling for stronger measures of control. The Wizard's Guild, of course, opposed. As the patrons listened, they murmured their assent.

The innkeeper's wife soon brought out a plate of food and set it before Karendle. "Here ya go! Those mages. I don't know!"

"How so?" Karendle asked.

"Some are nice enough, I suppose. But they're getting out of control, I say." She put her hands on her hips. "We had one try to rob us just last night!"

"Really?" Karendle asked, trying to hide the fact that she already knew, "What happened?"

16
Wizardry
Karendle

As she sat in the Brown Boar, finishing her dinner, she thought about how her life had changed in the last few days. Twynne Rivers was nothing like she had expected.

After getting thrown out of the Wizard's Guild, and after shouting angry dwarvish curses over the fence at the guards standing by the CenterTown wall, she had stormed away. It was evening, and darker than usual because of the heavy clouds that had drifted over the city. She started walking, but had not gone far when the rains began.

The first inn she found was quite expensive, and she only had a few coins. She tried offering work, cleaning, in exchange for a meal and lodging. One by one, the inns turned her back out into the rain. As she got further down the RiverFront the prices did get lower, but not low enough.

Finally, after talking to an innkeeper, she shook the rain from her clothes and started toward the door. As she passed two men sitting at a table, one of them gestured to her, "It looks like you're having a difficult time, eh?"

The other was more finely dressed, thinner, and had features that looked elvish. He called the innkeeper over. "Give her a room," he said, tossing three silver pieces on the table, "And a good hot meal."

She froze. "No, sir. I'm not sure who you think I am!"

The man laughed. "Not to worry. We'll not harm you. Sit down, miss." Then added, gesturing to the chair, "Please?"

He took charge of the conversation, asking her name, and telling her that he had seen her shouting at the Wizard's Guild at the gates to CenterTown earlier that evening. Her shock that she had been followed lessened as he explained that they also had problems with the guild.

As the innkeeper brought out their food, the elf explained that criminal wizards had become a huge problem in the city, but that the guild blocked all efforts to bring them to justice. He worked with a faction that wanted to put all of the rogue mages behind bars, and would she be willing to get back at the guild by helping them?

She hesitated. "How?"

"It's simple, really. By finding and capturing rogue criminal wizards, and bringing them to justice."

She was intrigued, but also suspicious. "And how would I do that, if I haven't learned any powers?"
The elf scoffed. "Who needs to learn magic? That's the long, hard way." He leaned in, and spoke more intensely. "I can give you the easy way to throw magic around. Are you interested?"

Her eyes opened wide. *I can use magic? Easily? It's always been so hard for me!* "I am! Tell me how that works!"

He reached back and grabbed a pouch and set it on the table next to her dinner plate. She slowly picked it up and peeked inside.

There were a number of gems, each big enough to fit in the palm of her hand. She reached in the bag, but the first man stopped her.

The elf explained, "We'd rather not have you display those here, for all to see." Nodding, she set the pouch back down on the table.

"Are they... Oculi?" She had heard of them from her father, who knew all about gems. She had never seen any like these, because the only ones that came to her city so far up in the hills were the ones on the river barges.

"Yes!" He explained, "Eyes of the Creator! With the red one, you can throw fire. With the blue one, you can move things using your mind. The grey ones? They're what you'll use to dimensionally entrap the foul mages that are sullying up our city. If... If, of course, you decide to help us."

He reached across the table and picked up the pouch with the oculi. Having finished their meal, and the conversation, the two men stood. The human put his hat on, and tipped it toward Karendle. "Miss, enjoy your dinner and your stay here. We'll talk more, tomorrow."

She had been unable think of anything to say as she had watched them step out the door and into the rain.

Back at the Brown Boar, she blinked her eyes, and came out of the reverie. She tossed a copper coin onto the table next to her plate and walked over to the stairs leading up to the rooms. As she passed the innkeeper's wife, she asked, "So, do you know where they took the wizard that your husband overcame?"

"I don't know." She put on a puzzled look, "Probably to the guard tower in the InnerWall, just down the sloping road a bit. That's the closest one, I'd think..."

Karendle smiled. "Thank you very much!"

"You're welcome. Bless your steps!"

17
Out In the Street
Thissraelle

Thissraelle stepped out of the inn, onto the street, and blinked up at the dull, gray, afternoon skies. The raining had stopped! She was happy about that. At first, it was thrilling to fly over the darkened city in the middle of the night with the rain in her face. Then, she felt the chill of the wet night air, and her will subsided and she had to land and look for shelter.

She had managed to get past the protection of the CenterTown walls, and had begun to walk through the silent shadowed streets. Before long, she found the glow of the oculus lamps on the main street of the RiverFront Quarter. It was still quiet, except for the rain, but there were lanterns shining through the windows of pubs and inns.

Her escape and wandering had taken much of the night, so once she settled into an inn, and a dry, warm bedroll, she slept long, way past the dawn.

This doesn't look so scary in the daylight! Yes, she had to admit to herself, in addition to being excited to be free in a new world, she also felt some fear. All up and down the street there was activity. Vendors pushing carts across the puddled cobblestones, women haggling over the price of a pig, and a man trying to coax a load, probably bags of grain, on to the back of an uncooperative donkey.

"You got copper?" The tiny voice jerked her gaze down. In front of her, there, no more than half her height, was a small human child, in ragged clothes. The child's long scraggly hair and unwashed face gave no clues as to whether it was a boy or a girl.

"I - I'm sorry?" Thissraelle stammered, off-guard.

The child held its open hand up higher. "You got copper?"

"Oh!" Thissraelle suddenly understood. "Yes! You poor waif!" She dug into her purse and pulled out two copper wedges, cut from a larger coin. She dropped them into the child's hand, who scurried away.

She stood, watching as the child vanished into the crowd and buildings. She had never seen anyone so poor before. *I hope there's a family for him. Her?* She stepped along the street, moving between vendors and residents, not really noticing the way they were looking at her.

She stopped abruptly when another child stepped in front of her. This one was a bit taller, a bit older, and her tattered clothing resembled a dress. She held out her hand and said, "Hey, you got copper!"

Thissraelle stepped back. She wasn't sure if that was a request or a statement. Maybe even a command. She reached into her purse as another child, a bit younger, rushed up and just started saying, "Copper, copper!" A third was following a short ways behind.

Thissraelle turned, and began to move more quickly in the other direction. The children followed, with their hands out. She grabbed some coins and wedges from her purse and tossed them to the side. As the kids scrambled to the ground to pick them up, she darted away, turning as quickly as she could.

The people on the street watched her go, then returned to their own efforts. Nobody noticed the one man who followed her.

18
The Confessor Priest
Antonerri

Antonerri was jarred from an uneasy sleep by a loud clanging. Startled, he shook his head and opened his eyes. Across the cell bars, next to the table stood two figures. They were mostly obscured by the dark and the incense smoke, but Antonerri knew who they were. One, a soldier guard, held a lantern low in one hand. It was swinging from side to side, jangling against the keys and tools on his belt, and casting shaking shadows around the room. The man's other hand swung back and forth, banging a sword against the bars of DeFrantis' cell.

"Get up, you!" He shouted in a scratchy voice, "Wake up! It's time to face your charges!"

Next to the guard stood a man in long, elaborate robes of fine white silk, trimmed in yellow and red piping. The robes bore elaborate embroidery of the emblem of the Church of Three Lights. He held a staff with a large, clear gemstone set in the head. He maintained his silence, glaring intently at Antonerri's huddled form. For a moment, their eyes met, and immediately the priest looked away, focusing on the other cell.

Antonerri looked to DeFrantis and saw her stir and sit up from the cold floor. She shook her head and ran her hand across her hair.

The soldier was losing patience. He banged his sword again. "Get up, you! On your knees before the Priesthood!"

She looked up at the priest, and Antonerri could see a shadow of fear cross her eyes, as she became fully awake and aware. Slowly, without removing her gaze, she knelt in the middle of the cell. He could tell already this was not going to go well for her. She needed to be strong, not timid. He shifted forward on the floor.

The priest spoke, "State your name!"

She dropped her gaze. "Are you the Confessor Priest?"

"SILENCE! I - ," He pounded the staff on the floor for emphasis, "I will ask the questions!"

She flinched and hid her face.

"What is your name?"

"DeFrantis." She whispered.

"Speak up!"

"DeFrantis. Of the OuterWall."

The priest snorted haughtily, and opened a small book carried under his arm. He held it in the light of the lantern and thumbed over the pages. "You are accused of thievery and robbery."

She straightened up, and reached out. "I didn't actually steal anything! I was attacked!"

"So, you are guilty, then?"

"I was only trying to feed the kids! They're hungry! There's no one to look after them!"

The priest pushed his shoulders back, raising the staff up higher. "I don't care! I'm not interested in your justifications! You are guilty, and you must be punished! Do you confess?" He stepped forward and hissed, "Do you also admit to being a practitioner of the Power of Shadow?"

Antonerri's mind raced. *Oh, no. This is bad. He's going to go off on her, and She's not going to be able to take this!* He rolled forward onto his feet.

She hesitated, "I -"

In a deep tone of righteous indignation, he intoned, "Are you a wizard of darkness?"

"No! I'm not!" She said, trembling, "I only know a little -"

"There is your confession!" The priest pointed the staff at her,

"So, feel the purging power of light!"

"No!" Antonerri lunged ahead and threw himself at the the bars, reaching through and grabbing the staff. A flash of light exploded in the room, coursed through his arm and body, and sent him flying back into his cell. The fierce pain in his muscles made it hard to breathe.

The priest's rage was quick. "How dare you interfere! Your punishment will be severe!" He pointed the gem at Antonerri and unleashed another blast of brightness. Antonerri screamed as the power rushed through him.

DeFrantis looked on in horror. "STOP!"

Antonerri rolled over and got up on his hands and knees. He struggled to stand as a third blast threw him up against the back wall of the cell.

"So, this is what happens when you intervene!"

Antonerri lay back against the wall, breathing heavily. His body could not move, shaking in pain. He looked at the priest, then at DeFrantis. *I tried. I tried to stop him.*

She rushed to the bars between them as if she wanted to break through them and comfort him. She looked at the priest and soldier in fear. He saw her eyes darting from one to the other. The soldier looked on with a smile, while the priest shouted latin curses and invocations at Antonerri.

"Yes, Father. I have sinned," DeFrantis said. He looked back at her in confusion as she kneeled by the bars before the priest. *What is she doing?* She bowed her head, "I need redemption."

58

19
Her Confession
Antonerri

What is she doing? Is she mad?

"It's all true." She spoke with a clear, determined voice. "I confess." The priest turned toward her, distracted from his ranting.

Antonerri saw her shoulders shaking behind her bowed head. Her hands were raised before her face, pleading for mercy. "I renounce the shadow! I embrace only the light! Please, Father, save me!"

No. Don't give in. Resist! But Antonerri had no strength to protest, or even call out.

"This is good, child, your punishment may be eased." Turning toward Antonerri, the priest declared, "You would do well to follow her example!"

She lunged forward, throwing herself down at the priest's feet and reaching for his robes. "Please, Father! I need redemption!"

The priest jumped back, unwilling to let his robes be sullied by her dirty hands. She shifted, and reached for the guard, grabbing at his tunic and leggings. "Please. I've been so wrong! My life is over! Help me be renewed!" The guard ripped his clothing from her hands and stepped back behind the priest. DeFrantis fell to the ground, shaking and sobbing.

The priest and the soldier exchanged glances, then with a nod from the priest, they stepped to the door. As they left, the soldier tossed a few more grains of incense into the bowl, which flared momentarily, adding to the smog in the room. Antonerri watched them go, then closed his eyes against the pain. He heard the door creak shut. Only silence remained. DeFrantis had stopped crying and was lying, curled up, on the floor.

After a moment, he saw her raise her head and look at the door. Then she looked at him and curled her lips into a faint smile. *What is she thinking? How can she confess?*

She rolled onto her back and sat up. She brought up her hand, pointing her finger. Dangling from it was the large ring of keys from the guard's belt.

In spite of his hurting, he shared her smile.

20
The Tower
Karendle

After her meal, she walked down the gentle slope of the hill, and found the wall separating the Inner and the Outer city areas. It was tall, possibly fifteen feet. It was built up of stone, and thick enough for a walkway along the top, complete with battlements. All along the wall was a wet cobblestone street, and opposite were houses and shops. The shops were starting to close up for the evening, and the people she passed were moving into the homes. As she walked along the street, she soon came to one of the guard towers built into the wall.

It was large and round, jutting out from the wall itself, with doors and windows. The tower was a few stories tall, much higher than the wall itself, with battlements on top. Upon finding it, she stepped into the door, and found two soldiers sitting at a table.

They were tall humans, especially compared to Karendle's own stature, each wearing a tunic with the emblem of the Twynne Rivers army. They stood right away and put their hands on their sword hilts.

"What are you wanting, now, miss?" One of them said, with narrow eyes full of suspicion.

"A - a young wizard was brought in here last night. A thief. I want to see her."

"Prisoners don't get visitors!" He barked, then reconsidered her. "What's your authority?"

She hadn't considered this question. She looked carefully at them both, "I've been given charge to track wizards in this city. I want to speak with the one you have captive."

"So you say. Show us your letter and seal. We won't just let anyone through here."

Of course. Those men didn't give me any authorization. And I should have asked to see theirs, too. What's their authority? Who hired them?
"I, ah, I don't have one yet."

The guards laughed and glanced at each other. "Well, you'd best be getting one, or we won't let you pass."

"Of course," She muttered, mostly to herself, "Thank you." She stepped back out onto the street.

21
Magic in Her Hands
Karendle

Karendle sat on the street, watching the guard tower. *How am I supposed to get in and get that mage? If she's captured already, should I still take her?* Her mind slipped back to the day after that first meeting in the inn. The two men had come back and found Karendle ready and eager. She could hardly keep her seat.

"Can I have the oculi?" She had asked as soon as they appeared. She reached out.

"Easy there, miss." One of them held back the pouch. "First, a couple of rules. Then, we'll have to show you how to use them."

She sat back, still impatient.

"First of all, you will tell no one about us. You will communicate with us using the blue oculus, but only when you have caught a mage, or are in dire need. And no-one can see you do it. Understood?"

She nodded, "How do I use the gem?"

"Calm down, we will explain all!" The other one also laughed at her impatience.

"Second, do not feel you need to ask questions of us. We will tell you what you need to know, when you need to know it. Dig no deeper than that."

That was a little troublesome, but she had nodded anyway.

"Good. Here." He tossed a small pouch to her. It jangled a bit as it hit the table. "That will get you started."

She opened the pouch and saw coins, easily five gold, and a few more silvers and coppers. She looked up, her eyes wide.

"When you bring us your first wizard, you'll get more." He stood and gestured to the door, "Shall we?"

She had followed them into the storm, to an isolated alley, and they had shown her how to hold the oculus. She had struggled at first, but was finally able to channel her will through it and shoot out a sharp blast of fire, which quickly fizzled in the rain. The memory of the thrill of feeling magic in her hand for the first time still made her tingle.

The next few days had been spent in her room at the inn,

practicing with the oculus. When she did get out, the constant rains meant there were few people, so she found no information about any mages. Finally, a pubcrier had announced another criminal wizard assault at an inn called the Brown Boar. Rain or shine, she would find this wizard!

As she sat remembering, an ornate white carriage rolled by and stopped in

63

front of the tower. It was pulled by a single horse, and the carriage and livery were all white. There was a symbol of three stars or lights on the side. *What's this?*

The driver set the brake, and climbed down to open the door. A man in white robes stepped out, then reached back in to get a long staff. He and the driver walked around to the door of the tower, being very careful to not step in any mud or puddles.

The driver opened the door and called out, "Please stand for the Priest Confessor!" The priest stepped in, and the driver returned to the carriage.

Karendle stood and walked down the street a bit further to get a better view. She'd seen the symbol a few times in the city. It was on a few of the cathedrals, and some of the soldiers wore it. She'd never seen it in the Dwarven Kingdom.

After a while, the Priest emerged from tower and called out to the driver, who scurried to open the door for his master. Karendle noticed that the priest looked agitated, flustered. *What could have happened inside?*

22
Watch The Street
Thissraelle

For the rest of the day, Thissraelle avoided children.

This left her conflicted. On the one hand, she wanted to help. *They are just children! They need a meal and a roof to sleep under!* But there were just so many of them, and they were so aggressive, it was more than a bit overwhelming. She struggled to understand as she walked the streets of the Twynne Rivers InnerWall.

I knew there was crime and poverty and suffering. I just imagined it happened to grownups. Isn't there some sort of shelter? An orphanage?

The streets meandered, lined by wood and stucco homes and shops, most of them two stories, occasionally separated by fences. The streets themselves were still wet from the rains, but drying. Most of them were paved in cobble, but many of the smaller side streets and alleys were dirt, now mud. There were many dogs trotting along the streets, and she thought she even saw some rats.

She walked past the working people, carrying heavy loads, leading carts and animals, sitting on the streets surrounded by food and wares for sale. Most wore rough and ragged clothing, cloaks and leggings. Many looked at her as she wandered.

Before long, she stepped down a street that opened up into a wide and busy walkway. As she moved forward she worked her way between passers-by and suddenly found herself looking over the expanse of docks and piers that lined the edge of the Wynne River.

She paused, struck by the sight. For years, she had seen it only from her tower window. It meandered through the town below her. Now, as she stood on the waterfront itself, it was much wider and stronger than she had imagined.

And much busier! People were walking up and down the piers next to barges and boats, loading and unloading. Carts and animals helped carry the heavier loads. She began walking down the waterfront, away from CenterTowne. She was fascinated by the constant motion. So much so that she almost ran into a man. She was startled and backed away.

"Oh! I'm sorry!" She stepped to the side, out of his way. He was a tall human, and wearing a dark shirt under a very black cloak.

"You look a bit lost." He said, and stepped into her way again.

"I'm... fine." This time she stepped away from him, a bit taken back by his imposition.

"You look like you're not from this part of the city." He took a step toward her.

"Excuse me, sir, I'm just passing along the street." She stepped back again. "I'm not trying to be in your way." She continued to back away.

She felt herself back into someone else, who immediately steadied her by grasping her shoulders. "Steady, there, miss," a man said, but didn't let go.

She tried to move aside, but he held her firmly in place. The first man moved forward again, so there was very little room to spare. She looked to her right, toward the buildings of the RiverFront, and saw a third man in a deep brown cloak walking forward, smiling and stealthily drawing a dagger.

He spoke, "You really shouldn't be in this part of town. Why don't you come with us?"

She felt her breath quicken, and her heart race. Her imagination ran to dark fearful places in her mind as she saw herself beaten, robbed, or worse.

Get control! Get strong! Breathe deep! Her fingers pressed to her temple, focusing her concentration. She dug deep into her will, gathered strength, and suddenly surged outward with her mind. The three men tumbled away from her, knocked off their feet by the force of the impact. Suddenly freed, she took a step backward and turned sideways, so that she could see them all and draw her own short blade.

The surprised passers-by lept aside and the three men scrambled to their feet and faced her. They all stood, facing off, as she started backing away. She glanced behind her and saw that she was only a few feet from where the dock drops straight to the river. She was cornered.

"She thinks she's a mage!" one of them taunted, but he was still a bit hesitant.

"I don't care!" Another said, "She's obviously got money!"

She tried to play it up. She stretched her hand out and said, "I WILL use my powers!" Her summoned confidence was doing a bad job of hiding the fear shaking her voice. "I Will!"

Someone on the street shouted, "A wizard! Run!" People started to scatter.

The man to her right laughed and lunged forward.

23
A Fight to Remember
Granthurg

The rains had finally ended, and the barge had arrived that afternoon in Twynne Rivers. As soon as they had claimed a pier and paid their fees, Granthurg and Rinkmorr uncovered their cargo and began to offload it. It was heavy, laborious work, but

Granthurg was accustomed to it. Once most of the crates, trunks, and bags had been loaded to the pier next to the barge, Granthurg began carrying it up to the quay, where the street ran along the river bank. There, Rinkmorr stood, and negotiated with the buyers and vendors as they passed.

As Granthurg was carrying a crate across his back, walking up the pier, his eye caught sight of a young girl on the wharf. She stood out, partly because she was dressed in a light-colored, finely-made cloak, which you don't see too often on the RiverFront, but also because he couldn't quite pin down her racial features. She looked elvish, but she was thinner, and her face was more angular than most elves he had seen here and in the forests. Her pointed ears stood out more. She walked with a step that was pleasant, almost haughty, and she was looking around as if she'd never seen a wharf or a waterfront before.

I know! She's a high elf! He'd only seen drawings of them in his scrolls, but once he made the connection, the facial features made him certain.

He leaned forward and shifted his load across his back.

When he got to the quay, he dropped his load near Rinkmorr, and glanced around. He couldn't see her. He shrugged it off and went back for another crate.

Back at the barge, he stretched his muscular shoulders and scanned the quay and the street again. *She must've gone into a shop. I wonder what she was doing down here by the river. I've never seen a high elf here in Twynne Rivers, much less in this part of town.*

His thoughts were interrupted by shouts from the street. He turned and looked and saw people scattering away from the girl, with her back to the river, staring down three full-grown human men. *Oh, she's in trouble!*

Granthurg reached to grab his hammer, and jumped off the barge onto the pier. His leap rocked the barge, so his footing slipped him to one knee on the pier. He jumped up and ran with thundering feet up the pier.

Rinkmorr saw him coming with the hammer in his hand and determination on his face. "Now, stop, there, Granthurg! What are you doing?"

Granthurg swung past Rinkmorr and ran up the street. He saw one of the men lunge at the girl and grab her at the waist, pinning her arms to her side. Another one stepped forward with a dagger. "Get her pouch!" He said.

Granthurg was on a full run at the moment, and had no time to slow down. He swung his hammer in front of him, but missed as the man dodged. Granthurg's momentum, however, carried him right over the stunned man, who crumbled under the weight of the Giant.

Granturg rolled off of him, as one of the others leapt onto his shoulders and tried to stab at him. Granthurg blocked the man's hands, then grabbed his cloak and used it to throw the man off of him, over his shoulder. He sat up, and looked for the girl. He saw her tangled in the assailant's arms. Then he saw her fade and dissappear, and in a rush, reappear a few feet away, free from the man's grasp.

Granturg felt a sharp pain in his shoulder. *Not again!* He swung his hammer around him, turning his shoulders and knocking the attacker to the street. The man struggled to gain his footing on the wet cobblestone as Granthurg stood and brought the hammer down in an arc above his head. The thief's eyes grew large and he rolled to one side as the hammer smacked into the stone below where his head was. A loud clang resounded and sparks chipped off the rock.

Granthurg looked up and saw the girl thrust an open palm at the one near her. A ball of light lept from her hand and exploded in brightness on the man's chest, sending him sprawling over the edge of the wharf and down into the murky water.

The other two thieves scrambled away.

Granthurg and the girl stood, staring at each other. She was defensive, not sure what to make of the Giant. Gradually, she eased and looked around her. The people on the street were staring at her with a mix of awe and fear. As she turned before them, they averted their own faces and scurried away. She dropped her face to the street, as if she were suddenly very self-conscious.

Granthurg took a deep breath and smiled. "I've never met a high elf before."

She looked up with her own smile. "And I've never met a giant!"

24
Another Escape
DeFrantis

"Hey! Wake up!" DeFrantis hissed as she leaned over and shook him gently. "Anto-- rini? --rooni? What is your name, again?"

She sat back. *Is he even alive?* After the confrontation with the confessor priest, he had just laid there in his cell. She had decided to let him rest. After taking the magical blasts, he was obviously hurt. That those blasts had been meant for her weighed on her mind.

She reached out and poked him, again. "Hey!"

This time, he stirred, and groaned. He rolled onto his back, and lifted his hand up to wipe his face. It looked like a painful motion.

"You ARE alive, after all."

He opened his eyes, and gradually focused. She stood, then leaned over him, offering her hand to help him up. He took it, and they pulled together. She had misjudged her stance and started to fall. She reached behind her, quickly, and grabbed the cell bars for stability. Now braced, she helped him up.

"I'm guessing it's probably night right now, so it'll be easier to escape." He let go of her hand, and stood on his own for a moment. His eyes finally fixed on the two open cell doors.

He smiled. "It looks like the keys worked," He mumbled.

"Can you walk?"

He just nodded and stepped toward the door. As she walked behind him, she glanced at the small table with the mage's bane incense burning in the bowl. She would be glad to finally be away from the smog it created, both in the air and in her soul.

The main room door was wooden, with steel banding as reinforcement. She paused in front of it. "I don't know what's beyond this door. Do you?"

He nodded. "There'll be a short hallway, and then the main guard room."

She slipped the key into the hole carefully, not wanting to make any noise. It clicked, but not too loudly. She pushed on the door and it began to swing out. It squeaked a little, and she stopped, took a breath, and then pushed again, more slowly. When it was halfway open, Antonneri stepped through. She followed.

A lantern in the guardroom cast a hopeful light down the hallway as they crept forward. They heard voices ahead, with a rattling noise. Antonneri turned around and gestured a shaking and tossing motion with his hands, then held up two fingers.

There are two of them, playing Lots. The air around her in the hall was a bit musty and smelly, and even still a bit damp from the rain, but she breathed it in eagerly. As it filled her lungs, she could feel it clearing her mind. She felt hope, and a bit of excitement. She nodded to Antonneri. *I'm ready!*

Antonneri nodded back, then turned and rushed into the room. DeFrantis immediately followed. Antonneri leaned under the heavy wooden table where the guards were playing, and flipped it up onto one of them. As the other stood, surprised, Antonneri swung his fist hard into the man's gut. The guard dropped, gasping for breath.

DeFrantis took in the room. It was circular, but not large. Opposite the table were two straw mattresses on the floor. Behind them, circling up the wall, was a stone stairway. *That's our freedom!*

"This way!" she called out as she darted to the stairway. Antonneri hit the downed guard across the back of his head, and he flopped to the floor, out. Antonneri stepped over him, then reached for his sword.

The other guard was pushing the table off as they started up the stairs. He called out, "STOP THEM! They're coming up!"

As she came to the top of the stairs, she saw another circular room about the same size, with two more guards leaping from a table and drawing their swords. This room had windows, and a large double door. Cool air wafted through the open window, and she took a deep breath. Her head was clear, now, her will and focus returning. She grabbed Antonneri's arm, then waved her other hand before her. She summoned her will and the darkness of the night flooded into the room, swelling up from the shadows on the floor until the entire room was shrouded. She heard the soldiers stumble and curse.

Antonneri's chuckle sounded behind her. "I thought you renounced the shadow." She yanked his arm and ran toward where she knew the door was. They hit the door, then Antonneri shouldered it. A third hit burst it open, and they stumbled out into the street.

"This way!" She shouted, even though she had no idea where she was. They hadn't taken more than a few steps when a bright explosion boomed just behind them, knocking them off their feet. Antonneri jumped up and ducked in between two buildings, with DeFrantis running scared behind him.

They ran through the alleyways, avoiding the streets, behind carts and crates and fences, until they finally collapsed, exhausted. As they gasped for breath, she got her bearings. *We're in the InnerWall, near the RiverFront.* She leaned against the wall and slid to the ground. With a groan, Antonneri sat beside her and they huddled in silence.

25
Cutting the Rough
Karendle

When she heard the first pounding on the other side of the tower door, Karendle jerked from her drowsy haze. She had been watching the tower all night, ever since the Priest had left. She moved from one side of the street to another, sitting here, standing there, trying to look like someone just waiting for a friend.

The second hit on the door made her jump to her feet and grab the bag of oculi. She dug quickly for the red gem, but it was hard to see in the darkness.

There was a third hit and the door smashed open. Two figures stumbled out. The first was a man in a white soldier's tunic that looked similar to the priest's robes. The second was a smaller figure in a dark cloak, possibly a girl. *I'll bet that's her! The mage!*

They scrambled to their feet, and the girl called out, "This way!" and they began running.

Wait! They can't get away! Instinctively, she jumped forward and reached out her hand, not fully realizing that it held the ruby oculus. As she pushed it forward with all her urgency, it sparked and threw a tiny burning ball of energy flying down the street toward the fleeing pair. The spark jarred her hand and knocked the oculus loose. As she fumbled to catch it, the energy ball exploded in a loud and bright blast, making her shield her eyes. The oculus and the bag clattered to the street.

After the blast there was a moment's silence. Karendle dropped to her knees. *Where did it go? I can hardly see!* She began to feel across the wet cobblestones. *Here it is!*

She felt the smooth stone of the street. *No, that's not it! They're getting away!*

Just as she grabbed the bag and found the gem, she heard more footsteps coming out of the tower. She scurried behind some barrels as they took off and ran away. Lantern light began to appear in windows up and down the street, and her eyes adjusted back to the darkness.

Muttering dwarvish curses, she ran after the fugitives.

Part 3

Together

26
Night on the RiverFront
Granthurg

Granthurg held out his hand to Thisraelle and steadied her as she stepped onto the barge. The afternoon sun had done much to dry the deck of the rains, and most of the cargo had been offloaded and either delivered or sold. He walked back to the stern platform and lit a lantern to chase the fading twilight.

"You don't use the oculi for light?" She asked as she stepped up onto the platform. "You have those large ones hanging up front."

"I don't know how." He shrugged. "Rinkmorr does. He hasn't taught me that yet."

"He's a bit rude, don't you think? He was upset that you helped me! He didn't even want to heal you!" She thought a minute. "And why doesn't he buy you a room at the inn? That's not right."

Granthurg laughed. "Someone has to watch the barge!. Oh, he's a bit rough, but he's good to work for. He's fair, and he pays me well." His hand massaged the soreness in his shoulder, where the wound had been. "The fact that he had to heal the same shoulder last night probably didn't help his mood much, either." Granthurg grunted as he turned a large chest on the deck to face him. He hefted it open.

"Here, take this. It's getting cold." He handed her a blanket from inside the chest. Then he flipped another blanket over his own shoulders. It was colorful, and large, but it barely covered his bulky shoulders.

By contrast, she was smothered in the one she was now wearing. "Well, I should have healed you, anyway, for helping me. I would have, but I was drained. My will is gone."

He reached back into the chest and brought out some scrolls. He gently set these on the floor of the platform near where Thissraelle was sitting. Then, he sat down in front of them and began to unroll them.

"That's something that Rinkmorr says a lot. I don't get it. I don't understand how magic and powers works." One of the scrolls was a map of Twynne Rivers and the surrounding area. He reached up for the lantern, and set it next to the map scroll. He began to study it intently. She found herself drawn to it as well, leaning over it.

His finger traced the line of the Greater Wynne River westward, past the shanties of the OuterWall, and over the rolling farmland to the Umbrawood Forest. He tapped the paper. "There. That's about where we were attacked." He carried on, thinking out loud, "But there's no settlements or even a lord's manor nearby. It's not too far from the forest... but..."

"What are you studying?"

"We were attacked by a couple of river pirates while travelling yesterday. I was trying to see if there was anything that might tell me where they came from. But I don't see anything."

He sat back, pondering, then looked at Thissraelle. She was staring at him, both confused and fascinated.

"What?" He asked.

"I'm sorry. I've never met a Giant, but I didn't think they'd be so..." She stopped herself.

He finished for her. "So studious? So... Smart?" She dropped her gaze.

"I'm very sorry. I really have a lot to learn."

Granthurg laughed. "Don't worry. I really am an odd one." He sat back. "As are you. I haven't been travelling the Wynne for too long, but you're the first high elf I've ever seen. You really looked out of place on the wharf. What brings you to Twynne Rivers?"

"Twynne Rivers is my home! I grew up here. I'm," She paused and got quiet, "I'm trying to get away from here."

A cold breeze blew through the silence between them. *That got awkward fast! There's a lot going on there that she's not talking about.*

He rolled up his scrolls and traded them for more blankets from the chest. "You really would be much more comfortable back at your inn. I can walk you back there."

She hesitated. "I'm fine. If you don't mind, I feel safer here."

They each spread out blankets on the hardwood deck, and before long, the gentle rolling of the waves had them each fully relaxed.

27
Night on the RiverFront, Part II
Thissraelle

It was dark, being night, but the lights of the street and the pubs up the wharf were moments of bright punctuation. It was noisy, too, and that was keeping Thisraelle awake. Her chambers at home had always been quiet. This was only the second night in her life she had ever slept anywhere else. That last time in her own room, only two nights ago, now seemed almost in another life.

80

"So," Granthurg's voice wafted over the deck, "You're a wizard."

She thought about that. Her father had taught her many things, but she had never thought of herself that way. "Yes, I guess I am."

"How does it work?"

She took a minute, unsure how to answer. "The powers are all around us. They always have been. Most people don't know it, and don't care. Some, like me, learn about them. We reach out and will that power to do things.

"But you said your will was gone."

"Yeah, you can only do so much. It drains you. Then you have to rest and recharge. As you grow, your will and knowledge increases, and you can do more things."

"It's kind of like having a flask of ale, then, right? Once you've drunk it, you have to get more!"

She laughed at the idea. "Yeah, I guess so. And just like there are different drinks, there are different kinds of power. There's Light, and, of course, Shadow. There's the power of Nature and life, as well as the power of the Mind. One of my favorites is Dimensional magic, but that one's tricky. Lastly, there's Striking power, using lightning or fire. My father taught me to use Light, Mental, and Dimensional powers. Eventually, I want to learn them all." She paused, then whispered, "I'm really pretty new at this."

Granthurg was quiet for a moment, "So, why doesn't running the barge upriver drain all of Rinkmorr's will?"

"I don't know. Maybe he's got an oculus, like the ones lighting up the front of the boat."

Granthurg sat up and looked toward the lights at the bow. Then he lay back down. "How do those work?"

She immediately thought of her father. "The oculi creatori? When a wizard creates an oculus, he'll infuse it with his own will. That power becomes a part of the gem permanently. Then, he can use it or draw from it."

"Hmmm. How do you make them?"

"I don't know. I've never done it. You have to be really experienced. Plus you have to have some pretty pricey gems. My dad used to buy them from the dwarves up in the mountains."

"Your dad is a wizard, too?"

She imagined her father finding out that she was gone. He would be very upset, and her Mother even more so. *They must be frantic about now.* She closed her eyes and tried not to think of them. "Yeah. He is."

28
Wizards are Trouble
Granthurg

The sun was shining on Granthurg's face when his eyes opened. It took him a minute to adjust his sight. He saw the blanketed form of Thissraelle sleeping on the other side of the barge's steering platform. There was a cool breeze blowing the smell of the early morning fish catch being cooked and sold off the wharf. The swirling air also carried the sounds of carts and people

82

starting their day along the RiverFront.

He rolled over and sat up. He was surprised to see Rinkmorr down on the cargo deck, a few feet away. Once they were in a city, Rinkmorr usually spent his days at the inns and shops, finding more cargo, and an occasional passenger. Here, he was kneeling in front of a large open chest. It was wooden, reinforced with iron straps and corners, and Granthurg recognized this as the chest where Rinkmorr kept all of his personal belongings. Rinkmorr was looking into a smaller wooden box that he had resting on some blankets and folded shirts inside the larger chest.

Before Granthurg could see what was in the box, Rinkmorr closed it and tucked it deep underneath the clothing and bags in the Chest. Then, with a heft, he swung the chest lid closed and locked it with a key from his pocket.

Granthurg called out, "Good Morning!"

Rinkmorr jerked, startled by the greeting.

"Oh!" He hesitated, "You're up!" He glanced at Granthurg and then back at the chest. He pushed it back into its place sternward on the cargo deck, then stood and walked toward the platform.

As he stepped up, he gestured to Thissraelle's still sleeping form.

"Look, what you do and who you're with is your own business," He whispered, "But be careful. She's a wizard. A lot of people don't like wizards. I like them less and less, the more I hear!"

"She's fine! She's just a lost elven girl."

"Yeah? Well, I trust elves even less than I trust wizards."

Granthurg thought about this, then smiled out of the corner of his mouth. "Wait. Aren't *you* a wizard? You use magic to drive the barge upstream. You've used it to heal me, and many other times, too."

"That's different! I'm a merchant and a riverman who happens to know a few tricks. She's a full wizard!" He paused and glanced back down at the chest, then gestured up at the city. "And don't get smart with me, either. Remember they pay me, and then I pay you. And they're not going to pay me to haul their goods if there's a mage on the barge. Especially that one, after that clash on the quay yesterday!"

Granthurg just stared at his boss, wide-eyed and surprised.

"Don't give me that look! Unless she's a paying passenger, get her off the barge!" Rinkmorr turned and stepped off the platform. He strode toward the loading plank. "With any luck, I'll have some good cargo by tomorrow and we can get back on the river! We've still got these few loads to take to PortsTowne as well."

Granturg watched him stride up the pier and onto the quay. *That's not like him to be so unfriendly! I wonder what got him so upset? We did really well with the loads this run, so it's not about*

84

money, unless he lost it all throwing lots...

Granthurg shrugged and bent to fold up his blanket.

29
We're Not Dead?
Antonerri

Antonerri could hear the harsh voice of the Sacerdotis Confesor echoing in the dark, heavy smoke of his cell. "How dare you interfere! Your punishment will be severe!"

The priest turned in rage and pointed his staff at Antonerri. "Your punishment will be severe!"

He shouted it again, "Your punishment *will* be *severe!*" The gem at the head of his staff glowed white. The priest shoved it at Antonerri, and a bright light leapt from the staff and shot directly at his upturned face. His eyes grew wide with fear as the shimmering brightness exploded on his chest--

Antonerri awoke with a jolt and a shiver. His eyes shocked wide open, the bright daylight surprised him. It took a few blinks for him to clear his vision.

He was sitting on cold ground, with his back leaning up against a home. At his left there were a couple of very large water barrels that must've given them some cover while hiding last night.

Hiding? Cover? What was I hiding from?

He looked to his right and saw DeFrantis sitting next to him, leaning on him. Her cloaked head was resting on his shoulder as she breathed quietly in her sleep. Her legs were curled up to her chest and tucked under the folds of her black cloak.

Another chilled breeze blew by and he shivered again. His mind began to clear and he remembered the escape of the night before: tipping the table, the explosion, the running, and finally the rest. *Once we rested, we must have fallen asleep.*

With the awareness came a stiffness of his back and shoulders, and harsh pangs of hunger.

He wiped his fingers across his eyes, then looked over at her. *She saved my life. That priest would have happily killed me. She could have left me there. Why did she think I was worth saving?*

She took in a sharp breath and lifted her head off Antonerri's shoulder. She shook the sleep out of her mind, then looked around, and settled her gaze on the face of her newfound companion.

"What...?" She stammered, "What happened? Where are we?"

She stretched out her legs and leaned away from the wall as she looked around. "We're still in the InnerWall, aren't we? We didn't get captured? We're not dead?"

"No, the one thing I'm certain of is that we're not dead." He laughed. "Not for now, anyway."

She smiled at him, then looked away. Suddenly, she jerked her head up, and scrambled to her feet. "The children! I've got to get back to the children!"

"What children? You spoke of them the other day, in the cell. What children?"

"Come on!" She pulled him up to his feet, and added, "We've got to get to the OuterWall quarter. They began running through the maze of streets, between carts pulled by animals and street vendors barking for attention. At each street corner, she would pause and look around, then she would grab Antonerri's arm and lunge off in another direction, until she began to get her bearings in the InerWall of Twynne Rivers city.

30
Where Have All The Children Gone?
Antonerri

Even though Antonerri had passed through the OuterWall quarter of Twynne Rivers several times, on his way in and out of the city, he had never walked its streets. They weren't so much "streets" as they were "the muddy spaces between the shanties" in kind of jagged lines. The roughly-made homes were dotted by occasional structures that were made into shops.

Antonerri and DeFrantis arrived in front of a small church. It was way too small to be called a Cathedral. It had the steeple, of course, and it was a solidly built structure, not like the rundown shanties. There was no abbey, or courtyard, just walls with a roof. The three glowing lights of the Church's emblem were painted on the door. The windows along the walls were mostly broken, and the outer walls were scraped and dirty. Clearly, this hadn't been used for worship for a very long time.

Cautiously, DeFrantis pushed open the front doors and stepped inside. Antonerri followed. The small chapel looked like it had been lifted up, turned upside down, and shaken before being set back down. There were pews, but they were scattered all over the space, mostly along the walls. In the empty center, there was a fire pit. All around the floor there was the clutter of more recent inhabitants.

Antonerri watched as DeFrantis began to call out names in the little chapel. "Where are you guys? Come on out!" She appeared to be more and more nervous, as time went on and nobody was appearing. She opened a door to what appeared to be a closet behind where the altar used to be, but found it empty as well.

"Nobody's here," She said, but it was less a statement of fact than an expression of confusion. "Maybe they're out begging, but if they were, someone would have had to stay back with Andrina."

Antonerri had also been looking through the chapel, but was unsure what he had been looking for. "Who lives here?"

"We do!" He could hear a bit of fear in her voice. "There's a whole group of us. Maybe a dozen or so. Most of them are children, under 10 winters old. They can't take care of themselves!" She turned to the main door and stepped outside. Again, Antonerri followed.

"This is just an old Three Lights chapel, not a home!" The warm sun on his face was a harsh contrast to the dark worry in DeFrantis' eyes.

"Well, we found it abandoned, and we made it our home. How can this happen? I was only gone, what, two or three days?" She spun around in the street in front of the chapel, looking one way, then the other. Finally, she sat down on a stone and started mumbling to herself. "If they were chased off, where would they go? They might be in the central circle..."

Antonerri also looked around, still not sure what he was looking for. He saw an older lady pulling a low cart full of breads along the way. The sun had been drying the ground some, but the path was still muddy, and making it rough for her to move the cart. Antonerri stepped across the street.

As he approached, the woman cowered and tried to pull her cart away. He stepped behind the cart and pushed it out of the muddy space and onto the drier ground of the main road in front of the chapel. Unsure what to do, she stood, surprised, and then began pulling the cart down the street.

"Pardon me," Antonerri spoke up, "Did you pass by this church during the rains these last few days?" DeFrantis looked up as well.

The lady stopped and adjusted her ragged shawl to cover her face more. "No. I was inside" She gestured to the structure she had been coming out of.

"Did you see any of the children that had been staying here?"

"Yes, I did."

Hearing that, DeFrantis jumped up and came to Antonerri's side. "What happened? Where are they? What did you see?"

The old lady spoke louder now, and a bit faster. "I saw a young man shouting at them to get into a cart with a horse. It was very strange. They climbed in, one by one. No coats or anything, in the pouring rain. Then another man tossed a tarp over them and

90

gave the young one a pouch. Off they each went, in different directions." She thought, then added, pointing, "The cart drove that way."

DeFrantis reached to Antonerri, and put her hand on his arm to steady herself. Slowly she slouched to her knees. Antonerri stood, unsure what to do. Finally, he spoke to the lady, thanking her.

"She doesn't look too good, does she?" The lady said, pointing at DeFrantis.

"No, she--"

The lady stepped toward her cart, reached in and brought out a couple of small bread loaves. "Here. She looks like this might do her good. Thanks for helping me."

He took the loaves and nodded, then watched as she led her cart down the street.

31
Money Talks
Thissraelle

Thissraelle walked beside Granthurg, looking at the ground. He was carrying a large load across his back, a couple of large sacks of grain tied together. She thought that would have been very difficult, but he seemed to be hefting it without straining. He was taking in the early afternoon of the city as he looked for the destination of the delivery.

Even though she had not met a Giant before, she saw a lot more of them on the Riverfront today. A lot of them seemed to run the barges like Granthurg did. They mingled with the populace, mostly humans, but with more than a few wood elves as well. Each was scurrying to get where they needed to be.

"Well, here we are!" He said and turned quickly to his left. He ducked his head low to push open the door of a building. From the looks of the sign, it was a baker's shop. The smells outside confirmed this. It was a small stucco hut, braced with huge wooden beams in the corners, and across the roof. She could see behind it a few large chimneys where the ovens were.

Moments later, he came back out with a smile and two large loaves of crusty, brown bread. He offered one to her. "Freshly baked!"

She took it and tore off a piece to eat, and they started walking back toward the RiverFront and the barge. She was silent as she walked, wondering what her next move was to be. Suddenly having all the freedom also meant too many choices. It was a bit dizzying. There was one thought, however, that had kept coming back to her. Finally, she spoke.

"How could I get to Emberfire?"

Granturg stopped, surprised, then smiled, "Ah, she speaks!"

"Yes, I can, in fact, speak." Thissraelle said. "Do your many maps say how to get there?"

They started walking again. "Emberfire is a city built into a mountainside some ways north of here. You could just get a horse and go through the Umbrawood Forest. It wouldn't be easy, but that would be the shortest way."

"Wouldn't that be dangerous?"

"Well, sure, Umbrawood is full of animals. Some are big and fierce, I suppose. But still, the wood elves travel to the city frequently, so I suppose you could take a ride in one of their caravans."

Thissraelle didn't like that option. "I think I'd be more afraid of the elves than the monsters in the woods!" That comment brought a sideways look from Granthurg.

She sighed. "The wood elves and the high elves don't get along very well, I'm told. I'm not entirely sure why. They fought each other in some historic war, maybe. I don't think they would take to kindly to helping me through their forest."

Granthurg considered that. "Well, you could travel east around the forest, through the grasslands of the felician tribes."

The thought of all that walking didn't appeal to her, but she didn't want to seem rude, either. She remained quiet.

"Or, you could sail west up the Lesser Wynne River to the towns on the north of the Umbramoor, and then hire a guide to take you along the base of the mountains eastward to Emberfire City."

Her bread was done about the same time that they stepped onto the pier where the barge was docked. She hesitated, looking down at the pier. "What if I hired passage on your barge up the Wynne? Would you take me to Umbramoor?" After a breath she added, "I'm sorry I got your master mad at you. I don't mean to be a burden. But, he did say that I could pay passage, didn't he?"

"He did say that." Granthurg helped her onto the barge. "But it's pretty expensive. It can cost a couple of gold pieces to go all the way upriver."

Thissraelle reached into a small pouch and pulled out three gold coins. "Well, then, this should about cover it, then!" She dropped them into Granthurg's hand and stepped past him and took a seat on the steering platform. "When do we leave?"

"Well, we'll want to pick up some cargo that will be going that way as well, so it might be another day or so."

"No matter. I'm not in a hurry." She smiled. "Now that we're here, would you show me those maps again?"

32
Back at The Chapel
DeFrantis

DeFrantis threw open the door behind the altar in the small chapel and began scattering the small boxes and other debris stored there. She pushed blankets and old sacramental robes aside until she cleared a corner of the bare floor. She looked at the tiles for a moment, trying to remember which one held her prize.

Antonerri came in behind her. "What are you doing?"

She ignored him, but simply began tapping lightly on the floor tiles. At random, at first, but then, when she got no results, she started on one side and methodically moved from one to another.

"I've figured some things out in the few days I've known you, but if you want my help, it might be useful to tell me what's going on."

"You don't need to come with me." She said, in a brusque tone. "They are in grave danger and they need me."

"Who are 'they'? What are you looking for?" He stepped forward. In that moment, she started clawing at a dusty tile, but she couldn't get under it.

She grunted in frustration, then looked around. Seeing Antonerri standing near, she said, "Give me your sword!" She held out her hand.

He flipped it around, holding it carefully by the blade, and placing the hilt into her open palm. She grabbed it and, using both hands, easily wedged it under the tile and pulled it up. She flipped it aside, revealing a hole underneath. Setting the sword down, she leaned over the hole and reached deep into it. She came up with a small pouch.

"What's that?" Antonerri asked.

She stood up and climbed over the clutter past Antonerri to exit the small room. He followed her out into the main hall.

"DeFrantis!" He called out. She was already halfway through the door when she stopped and turned.

"What?"

"What's the big secret?"

"It's not a secret! I'm just focused. I'm worried."
"About the kids?"

Her shoulders, at first held back in defiance, slouched. "Yes."

"Who are they? Where are they?" He stepped toward her, off the dais of the altar. When he reached her, he said, "Look, you don't know me, but in the tower you saved my life. You could have left me there to rot once you got the key. But you brought me out."

"Well, you took the blasts from the priest that were meant for me! I couldn't leave you there."

He put his hand on her shoulder. "OK, then. Let me help you now."

She sighed and sat down.

"I've lived on the streets of the OuterWall most of my life, since I was barely 12 winters old. I learned to live off of scraps and how to avoid trouble. Gradually, I teamed up with other kids my age. As I got older, most of them left off on their own, but more young ones came to me. I took care of them, taught them to protect themselves, to beg, to survive.

"There was one boy who was with me most of those years. He was mean and hard, but he did his part to help take care of everyone.

"One day, not long ago, he told me that someone had offered him money to take the children off to the Umbrawood forest to the west. He tried to talk me into doing it. He said they'd be safe and they'd be out of our way. He said they'd offered a gold piece a head."

Antonerri looked shocked.

"I was appalled! How could he even think of that? I told him there was no way I'd sell these kids out. How can I sell what I don't own? Plus, they were probably slavers or worse. I couldn't do that."

"Then, when the rains came these last few days, and there was nobody to beg from, I set out to see if I could scrounge a meal. I ended up being captured and held under the tower with you."

Antonerri finished the story. "And now, it seems that your friend has sold them away."

She stood up. "I have to find them! I have to help them!"

"What's that in your hand?"

"Some silver pieces I've saved. Hopefully, we can connect with a caravan or a barge travelling west to get us to the forest to search for them." She held it out so he could see the bulging coins. "You don't have to come. This isn't your problem."

He gestured to the chapel above him, and said, "The Church that once gave me purpose and belonging now considers me a criminal heretic. I have nowhere to go."

She nodded, and they walked from the chapel.

33
Lost and Found
Karendle

By the time she was tired of looking for her quarry, the sun was hanging a bit low, tinting the building-tops of the InnerWall with orange.

The night before, she had seen them escape the guard tower, and even managed to knock them to their knees with an ill-planned explosion of magical power from her oculus. That woke the soldiers on guard as well as the neighborhood. She tried to rush off after the two fugitives, but the soldiers saw her move and began to pursue her, instead. This was only made worse by the people who heard the bang and came running out of pubs and homes to see what was going on.

In the unfamiliar city, it hadn't been easy for her to lose the soldiers. Fortunately, there were many roads and alleys for her to disappear into. She spent the night in fitful sleep under awnings and behind storage barrels, waking and moving frequently.

As the morning sun was starting to show a faint glow in the sky, she finally found a stable with a pile of straw and sank into exhausted slumber.

She awoke just before midday, and slid back out into the street. It was busy enough and she managed to blend her way along, still avoiding any contact with soldiers or constables.

After a meal at an inn, she had wondered what her next step was. She could keep searching for the same wizard and her soldier friend, or try to find another wizard to capture. For now, she decided to resume her search. She would retrace her steps of the night before. It was difficult at first to find the same guard tower, and, after following the direction of everyone's flight into the depths of the city, it became clear that she had lost any real chance of finding the wizard. It was as if the girl and her friend had blended into the city's shadows.

Unwilling to give up, she had spent the afternoon wandering the the streets of the InnerWall and finally found herself on the northern wharfs of the RiverFront.

By that time, it was getting to be early evening, and she sat down on a public bench, weary and needing a rest.

98

This is much harder than I thought. There are so many ways for someone to vanish. I'm quite hungry as well, but I need to be careful with my coin. She opened up her purse and reached in, shifting the oculi aside to find a few gold pieces remaining. *I guess I'll be OK. I just want to bring back a wizard. I want to make this happen!*

As the sun began to lower, she stood and walked upriver, only casually glancing around her. *A fried fish at a pub here on the river would be pretty nice, right about now.*

As she stepped toward a pub she walked past a couple of open air tables by the side of the river. Around them were seated giants, river runners, and barge steersmen, talking and sharing ale. While most were talking among themselves, a few were talking with others, non-giants. As she passed she could hear them talking about cargo rates and passenger fares. A lady seemed to be booking passage to the west.

She walked on, then paused. *That woman's voice. I've heard it before.* Karendle turned to look back at the table. One of the giants, bulky, with a shaved head and a vest, was walking down the pier toward the barges. With him walked a man in white soldier's livery, with a diminutive woman in a black cloak. In an instant, she recognized them! *That's her! I can't believe my luck!*

She quickly reached for her purse, and rushed back. Before she got to the table, she paused. *Oh no. There are a lot of people here. I'm not making the same mistake twice!*

She watched as they all boarded one of the barges. *I'll just take my time and watch. Maybe tonight the situation will be better.*

She backed away and found a small barrel to sit on, and waited.

"Thurg!" a sharp voice hissed through the night on the wharf. "Thurg!" it sounded again, louder.

Granthurg was sitting at one of the tables on the wharf, studying scrolls by lanternlight. He looked up, then turned toward the voice. "Rinkmorr?"

"Hush! Come over here! Leave the Lantern"

Granthurg stood and stepped out of the circle of light around the table. His face, now obscured in shadow was furrowed and confused. "Where are you? What are you--"

"Quiet, boy! This is critical." Granthurg could barely make out the massive form and familiar face of Rinkmorr hiding behind some large covered crates on the wharf. Before he could speak, Rinkmorr interjected, "Who's that down on the barge?"

"Passengers. I've been excited to tell you. I've booked passengers! They've paid half up front, like you always--"

"I thought I told you to get rid of the elf girl."

"She's paid her fare in full!" Granthurg was quite pleased with himself. "In gold! The others just booked on board, too. They're all going west, up the Lesser Wynne River. I told them we could get sailing really soon, as soon as you get new cargo!" He held up a small pouch and jingled it. Rinkmorr took it and hefted it before pocketing it.

"Yeah, well, never mind that. West, huh? Well, west is good!"

"West is Best!" Rinkmorr rolled his eyes at Granthurg chanting the old Riverman's adage. Going west usually meant going home.

"Thurg! Listen to me, and listen close." He reached out and grabbed Granthurg's shoulders and held him looking forward, into Rinkmorr's worried eyes. "I need you to do something important. I need you to take the barge and float it tonight. Upriver, west will be perfect, now that I think of it. Drive it right away." He paused, and looked behind him.

"But we have no cargo! We have few supplies!"

"That doesn't matter. Just take it tonight."

"Wait. Does that mean you won't be on board?"

"You wanted a chance to be a riverman, right? Now you can be! Take it all the way up to Umbramire port and wait for me there."

Granthurg was shocked and confused. "What's happening? What's the rush? Are you in trouble?"

Rinkmorr's silence confirmed this. "What did you do?"

"I owe some people some money, that's all. Nothing you have to concern yourself about. It's just that some people might come to collect by taking something I have, and I need it to be gone. That's why you have to leave right away."

"Did you lose the barge throwing lots?"

"That's not your concern. But, no. Now, get out of here!" Rinkmorr was already moving away.

Granthurg followed him for a few steps "I don't know how to drive the barge upriver! I don't know the magic!"

"Get your girlfriend to figure it out! The oculus is in the stern. Now get out of here before they see me! Don't let me down!"

"Rinkmorr!" But the elder giant had already slipped away in the darkness. *Well, he's got some nerve! What do I do now?* Granthurg stood, trying to see across the wharf. Finally, he returned to his scrolls and rolled them into his carrying pouch.

And she's not my girlfriend, either...

35
Headin' Out, A Little Early
Granthurg

Granthurg dropped the scrolls into his trunk and closed the lid. He locked it, and pushed it back out of the way on the deck. All the while his mind was racing with questions. *I don't understand. This isn't right. Why do we need to leave right away? We still have a few pieces of cargo we haven't offloaded!*

He shivered. The night was cold, and he felt it more than usual. He stood, turned and almost knocked Thissraelle over. He steadied her, stepped back, and looked down. She had a concerned look on her face.

"Sorry." He moved around her and walked past his other passengers toward the steering platform.

"Granthurg! What's wrong?"

He kept walking, taking a step up onto the platform. "Granthurg!" She insisted.

He knelt by the steering oar at the stern and reached behind it, feeling for the lock he knew was hidden there.

"Granthurg! What's going on?" She grabbed his arm and turned him toward her. "Look, I've only known you a few days, but you look like you're upset."

He nodded, then reached around again, and pulled up the rusty chain and lock. He pulled his keys out of his pocket and unlocked it. "We have to leave. I don't know what's going on, either, and that's probably why I'm upset." He pulled the chain free, then backed up on his knees. She followed. He swung open a small trap door, about the size of a couple of the deck planks. The lantern light above shone in and reflected off of something inside.

"There it is. Now if I can only figure out how to use it." It was a stone, about the size of a human's fist, of fine, polished jade. It was mostly green, but had some veins of brown running through it.

She leaned over to look, and recognized it as an Oculus Creator, infused with the powers of nature. "This is what Rinkmorr uses for the power to drive the barge upriver, just like I was saying."

"Tonight he told me he needs us to leave, and go west. Something very bad is going on, and I don't know what. Some people are after something he has. I don't even know how to make this thing work." He paused, then looked at her intently, "Do you?"

"I don't know natural magics, but I've used oculi lots of times. I could try."

He smiled for the first time that night. "Thanks. That's all any of us can do."

"What did Rinkmorr do to make it work?"

Granthurg chuckled, "He'd just sit there with his eyes closed, looking like a doof, and the boat would go. Then, when it was moving, he'd get up and steer like normal." Granthrug stood. "Give it a try. I'll get the barge ready."

She reached in and felt the stone. Granthurg walked back toward the bow, and began to undo the mooring. He called out to the other passengers, resting on the cargo deck. "I hope you good folk don't mind, but we've had a bit of change in plans. We'll be casting off and heading up the Lesser Wynne tonight."

DeFrantis and Antonerri glanced at each other, and DeFrantis spoke, "For us, the sooner we leave, the better."

"Oh, no. No, no, no." A deep voice from the pier surprised them. "You're not leaving quite just yet." Granthurg's head snapped around to see three men standing on the pier, bathed in the light of the fore oculi. They were cloaked in dark colors. The leader was quite tall, even for a human, and his long, scraggly hair covered much of his face. He jumped onto the barge, along with his two companions. Granthurg stepped back, defensive. He looked back at Thissraelle, and saw his hammer sitting on the deck near her. He looked back at the men.

The leader spoke again, with a menacing gravel, "Of course, if you just give us what is ours, then we can all be on our way as soon as you like."

36
A Quest!
Eddiwarth

There were about two dozen novices having their evening meal together at the tables in the Wizard's Guild school hall. They were talking and laughing, creating a low level of noise that filled the air like the thin smoke from the hearthfires burning in the center of the room. The fading afternoon light still shone through the ornate windows, but oculi mounted around the room provided most of the light. Occasionally, one of the students would get up from the table, cross to the fire and refill his bowl from the stew brewing there.

Eddiwarth was one of the louder ones, laughing and shouting with his classmates. He had only been at the guild for about a month, and had quickly tried to fit in. While his constant pranking and joking had rubbed many the wrong way, there were a few that enjoyed watching him embarrass other students and then take the fall for it. As a result, he didn't have many friends, but there were some who were willing to associate with him, more out of a desire for entertainment, than real friendship.

He was a half-elf, born and raised in Twynne Rivers, the son of a high-elf merchant and his human mother. His father's marriage meant they were disallowed in the city's high-elven community, and his impulsive nature meant he never was able to focus long enough to learn a trade. The only thing he was any good at was a few bits of magic. So, as he came of age, his father managed to convince some others to use some connections and he was reluctantly accepted into the guild.

He didn't notice when the Class Master Faloren came into the room. Quickly, the talking hushed as the lanky Master slid between the tables to stand by the fire. He turned to face the class as it all got quiet.

Just in time to hear Eddiwarth shout, "...So he said, 'OK, but this time YOU put the dress on the ox!'" It took a moment after delivering the punchline for Eddiwarth to notice that he was the only one laughing at the joke. He quickly sat down, while others rolled their eyes and snickered.

Decorum restored, for the moment, Faloren spoke.

"Our great GuildMaster has sent me here tonight with a command. A rather odd command, I believe, but I will fulfill it, nonetheless. He wishes me to recruit a few volunteers for a quest of great importance." Here he paused, as if it drew great pains for him to proceed. "I'm not at all clear as to why he would want to recruit for so important a task from such a pathetic collection of rabble as you all. It is beyond my capacity for understanding. And my understanding is truly vast."

He breathed deep. "At any rate, he wishes two to three of you to go and risk your miserable lives in this quest. As with most tasks and quests you will likely undertake in your wizardic careers, success will bring with it the gratitude of the GuildMaster, and all the prestige that entails, but no actual treasure or payment. Failure, will, of course, probably bring shame on you and your family, probably posthumously, etc, etc, etc..."

A voice, trying to remain anonymous, called out, "What's the quest?"

Faloren sighed. "If I were at liberty to tell you, I would have already done so." He clapped his hands, and called out, "So! Who wants to go?" His face brightly beamed with sarcasm and disdain.

The fire crackled and popped as the novices all looked back and forth at each other, wondering who would volunteer. Finally a young man stood and stepped forward. "I will go and bring honor to my class and family." He was a thin, but tall human in his late teens, dressed in a white shirt of fine linen. His hair was light, long and carefully combed, and he sported the thin beginnings of a beard.

"Ah, Master Hamrisonn. Of course you will." Faloren intoned.

"OH YEAH!" Eddiwarth jumped up. "I'll go, too! This'll be great! We'll get it done!" He rushed to the side of the other volunteer, shouting and waving his fist in the air.

The other students broke into pandemonium, laughing and clapping. Pleased to be rid of both of their cohorts, their cheers were, at least, sincere.

Faloren simply gestured for the two to follow him, and turned on his heel.

37
Find the Girl
Eddiwarth

Faloren was older, and his gait was deliberate, but the two young men had to both hustle to catch up. Eddiwarth was the first to speak up as well.

"So, what's this quest? What's so important?" His mind raced with scenes of battling dragons and seizing treasures. "Oh, I know! The wood elves are mustering for war, and the GuildMaster wants us to deliver an urgent diplomatic message to them! No! Wait - an ancient relic has been discovered, and we're to go and retrieve it!"

Faloren stopped and faced them. "You impudent twits really have no idea what's going on, do you? Personally, I wouldn't trust you with any task more difficult than fetching me an ale, and you still wouldn't get that right!" He resumed walking.

"The GuildMaster's daughter, Thissraelle, is missing. You've seen her many times here in the Guild Hall, I'm sure. The GuildMistress is beside herself with fear and worry. The Master is more calm, but is upset, nonetheless. We don't know if she was taken or if she just left on her own. For some reason, he wants someone from your class to go and retrieve her. Something about not being able to spare more experienced members, and it being a 'good learning opportunity' for you." The old teacher waved his fingers in the air to emphasize the quote.

108

Eddiwarth's classmate spoke. "How long has she been missing?"

"It was discovered yesterday morning, when she didn't arrive for breakfast with her family." He stopped in front of a door, and willed it to move. It slowly swung open and a breeze of the evening air wafted into the hallway. He stepped into the main guild courtyard, where he stopped. He could have opened the door with his hands, and that would have also been easier, in many ways, but he liked using his powers in front of the novices. It helped show them who was in charge.

Eddiwarth didn't notice. He started straight for the main gate out of the guild hall and into the city. Hamrisonn chased after him. "Hey, wait! There are more questions!"

Eddiwarth turned around, with a look of exasperation. "Go on..."

"Well, where was she in the guild hall last? Where might she have gone? Do we have any ideas who might have taken her?"

Faloren said, "She has been seen in the InnerWall, near the RiverFront."

"Seen? By who?"

Faloren thought to himself, debating. Finally, he decided to say. "The Guild has oculi hidden to see visions from all over Twynne Rivers." He enjoyed the look of surprise on the novices' faces. He walked past them toward the gate. "Really, you think they're the Eyes of the Creator, but a lot of them are also the eyes of the Guild."

He paused and signaled to the guards to open the gate. He handed a small jingling pouch to the two novices, and said, "Find

her. Bring her back quickly. Then you can return to your studies."
He gestured to the gate. "If you're still alive, that is."

"Go." He added, as they hesitated. "Now!"

38
What is Going On?
DeFrantis

"This doesn't look good," DeFrantis said, scowling at the ruffians
at the barge's bow.

Antonerri raised up and looked over the cargo crates and bags
stacked on the deck. The three men had just stepped off the pier
onto the barge and began moving aft along the walkway beside
the cargo. The way the Giant stepped back defensively was
telling. They weren't too far away, so DeFrantis and Antonerri
could hear the conversation easily in the otherwise quiet night.

"What is it you're looking for?" Granthurg asked.

"Oh, don't play like you don't already know!" One of the men
jumped up on some cargo boxes and began to move across them,
toward the stern, toward DeFrantis. He was looking closely at
each crate as he crawled over it. The other two reached into their
cloaks and drew out short swords.

"Oh, this is definitely not good." DeFrantis whispered. She saw
Antonerri grip his own stolen sword more tightly, keeping it
hidden from the view of the assailants. "What have we gotten
ourselves into?" *I don't know who's good or bad, here. Granthurg's
been very kind and he gave us a good price on our passage, but he looks
to be tangled up in some real problems!*

The apparent leader jabbed his sword at Granthurg, who jumped back. "Hey, easy, there..."

"Just tell me where it is, and nobody has to get hurt!" The ruffian jerked his head a bit, signaling his companion. The other man ran around the boxes to the other side of the barge, heading toward the stern.

The giant staggered backward, calling out, "Thissraelle! Get the barge moving!" He was trying to get to her without losing sight of the ruffian leader threatening him. The man followed Granthurg, holding his sword steady before him.

What to do? Where's the other one? DeFrantis strained to see, then glanced with worry at Antonerri. He was intently watching the drama at the side of the boat unfold. As the giant stepped past him, Antonerri spun and lunged at the intruder, knocking him off his feet into the railing. The two of them tumbled to the deck. Granthurg and DeFrantis both looked on for a moment, surprised by the attack.

"GRANTHURG!" A high voice called out from the stern. Granthurg and DeFrantis both turned their heads to see a huge double-handed warhammer floating quickly through the air, guided by Thissraelle's powers. He reached up and grabbed it,

111

then reset himself for the battle.

Out of the corner of her eye, DeFrantis saw motion. The other assailant was rushing aft, and was almost to the steering platform where Thissraelle was standing. DeFrantis quickly reached into her own will. She raised the shadows around the crates and the pier, drawing them upward, into the air They twisted around the ruffian, binding him fast in darkness. Thissraelle looked at her in surprise, then smiled quickly, and jumped back to her task with the oculus under the platform.

Just as quickly, DeFrantis was knocked to the deck as another assailant landed on her from behind. She wriggled and struggled beneath him, feeling a sharp cutting pain in her arm. As she struggled, she found her face pressed to the floor as fingers twisted into her hair and pulled her head back. She saw the brief flash of lantern light reflected off a bloody dagger in front of her face.

I'm going to die!

Another heavy weight hit her and the man on her back,

slamming them both flat. It knocked her breath out and smacked her head onto the deck. In another instant, the others rolled off her back and she could breathe again. She looked and saw Antonerri wrestling her attacker to the deck. Who had the advantage was not at all clear, though.

She tried to lift herself up, but one hand slipped on something wet and warm. She looked at it and saw blood. The arm hurt, too, higher up toward the shoulder, and it felt weak. *Is that my blood?* She managed to lift herself up with her other arm. She could hear the clang of the sword on the hammer to her left. To her right, Antonerri was on his back trying to fend off fist blows being thrown to his face.

The barge lurched in the water and, with a loud crunch, banged against another craft berthed beside it. The impact flipped DeFrantis over onto her back. The barge lurched again, as it began to move away from the pier.

She felt dizzy, and that made it hard to get up. She could feel her will slipping away, releasing the shadows holding the third man. She tried to maintain their strength, but finally had to let them dissipate. .

What did we get ourselves into?

39
Who is Who?
Karendle

Noises from the barge jolted Karendle awake. She lifted her head up from the table on the wharf where she was sitting. She had been watching the giant and the barge diligently, but had drifted off to sleep at some point in the early night. She stood up and looked down the pier, and saw three strange men on the barge fighting with the giant and the others. *Hey, who is this?* She saw one of them jump at the dark-cloaked wizard girl. *They're after my quarry! I've got to stop this!*

With a leap, Karendle took off running. Her sleepy grogginess and the swaying of the pier made it a bit difficult for her to maintain her balance. As she got to the barge, she was about to jump on board, but was surprised to see it suddenly lurch in the water, smashing into another nearby barge.

She regained her balance, took a step back, and threw herself over the widening gap of water, landing hard on the foredeck.

She scrambled to her feet, and looked aft over the cargo crates. *There's the giant, fighting one of the men, and there's another that looks like he's tangled up in darkness. That's got to be the doing of the girl I'm after! But where is she? I can't see over all this cargo!*

She jumped up and clambered to the top of the pile of crates. From there, she could see much better. *I need to get my oculi ready this time!* She grabbed her pouch, then looked out over the scene. The wizard girl was lying on her back, and she didn't look good. Next to her two men were wrestling, and beyond them, the man who had been wrapped in darkness was free and jumping to his feet. He seemed to be rushing toward the stern where a young elven girl was sitting in lantern light.

A sudden loud whoop of laughter from above caught everyone's attention. Seemingly out of the dark sky, into the wash of the light of the lanterns and oculi, a young man, or maybe an elf, floated quickly down onto the deck in front of the platform. He spun toward the man rushing aft and shouted, "Oh, no, you

114

don't! She's mine!"

He pointed, and a hot pulse of fire shot from his hand, hitting the surprised ruffian squarely on the chest. The flash burst brightly and loudly, blasting him up and off the barge. He splashed hard into the Wynne. The Elf girl screamed.

Karendle dropped to the crates, trying to hide. *My Holy Lights! Another Wizard! This IS my lucky day!* She looked again. There was something familiar about the pattern of his red and blue shirt that she had seen before. *Not the colors, but maybe the patterns or the markings?*

A sudden wave hit the barge, and hit it hard. It flipped everyone off their feet, and onto the deck. Karendle landed in the now loose pile of crates, then scurried to regain her balance.

The Elf screamed again, and yelled something Karendle didn't understand. She raised herself up to see. The barge was stable in the water, and everyone was climbing back to their feet. All except the girl, who was being held tight by yet another young man, this one definitely human, and wearing clothing similar to the other wizard. He gripped her around her waist, his sleeves and arms glowing white with bright light.

"Hold still!" He yelled at her, "We're just taking you home!"

She shouted and kicked at him, to no avail. Then she stopped, and seemed to focus her mind. There was a sizzling, crackling sound, and in an instant they were gone. It was as if reality itself swallowed them both and gulped them down.

THISSRAELLE!" a deeper voice screamed. The giant lumbered to where the elf had been on the platform and fell to the deck.

For a moment, everyone on the barge just looked at each other. No one seemed to know who anyone else was, or why they were there. All except the giant, who was frantically looking around trying see where the elf girl had gone. The shadow wizard girl and her friend were pretty badly beaten up, and looked like they didn't know who they were fighting, or why. Their attackers were looking at the fire wizard in the middle of the boat like he was some sort of avenging angel, and he wasn't there to rescue them. Suddenly something clicked in Karendle's mind.

They're from the Wizard's Guild! But that revelation brought more questions. *What are they doing here? And why do they want the girl?*

She reached into her pouch as she scrambled to her feet. *Well, I don't care! I'm here to catch wizards, and I hate the Wizard's Guild, so that's all the understanding I need!*

She pulled out the entrapment oculus, and pointed it at the fire mage in the middle of the barge, shouting, "I'm taking you down, wizard!" Surprised faces turned to look at her as the oculus glowed with silvery light, which grew and quickly enveloped the man. The light surrounded him, then shrunk around him, shrunk with him, and finally sucked him into the glowing stone.

Karendle looked at the grey gem in her hand and mused, "Amazing! It worked!"

The silent confusion was shattered by the giant's grunts of rage as he rushed at the man who had attacked him, swinging his hammer before him. "Get! OFF! My! BOAT!" He landed a solid hit, smashing the man into the railing, which broke and sent him tumbling into the river.

The soldier in the white tunic rolled from his prone position on the deck to grab his sword and slash the legs of the ruffian who had been beating on him. The man screamed and fell to the deck, where the soldier kicked him off the other side of the barge. The soldier then crawled over to the shadow mage, and helped her sit up. They, Karendle, and the giant looked from one to the other, in awkward and confused silence.

That silence, moments later, was broken by a crackling sound from the bow of the boat. As everyone looked, reality again distorted and swirled, finally spitting the elf girl, screaming, out onto the deck, sprawled across a few of the cargo crates.

"Thissraelle!" The giant ran to her and lifted her up.

"Thanks!" She shivered, clinging to his warmth, "Can I get a blanket?"

As the elf girl made her way to the steering platform, the soldier in white asked, "What happened to the one who had you trapped?"

She smiled, "I left him in The Vast." Karendle didn't understand, and obviously neither did anyone else. "I'll explain later."

The giant wrapped Thissraelle in a blanket, before climbing onto the platform and steering the barge out over the dark river. Karendle saw her shiver and wrap herself up in the blanket's soft comfort, then stepped over to the shadow girl.

The big giant returned aft and stepped up to the steering platform and sighed, "West. West is Best."

41
And Who Are You?
Granthurg

For the last hour, Granthurg had steered the barge westward in silence. He looked down at Thissraelle, wrapped in a blanket on the platform at his feet, fast asleep. After using her powers of light to heal DeFrantis' shoulder, she had collapsed in exhaustion. Antonerri and DeFrantis sat together on the deck, huddled together, too tense to sleep. They weren't talking, but just looked at Granthurg and the unknown other woman, who sat between them and to one side.

Granthurg noticed that she was also nervous, and shifting her gaze back and forth between the giant and the others. Granthurg leaned forward and picked up a bundle of blankets. He stepped away from the rudder and off the platform. He offered blankets to Antonerri and DeFrantis. Antonneri wrapped one around DeFrantis' shoulders.

118

Granthurg hesitated and looked at the unknown lady. She looked not quite human, but was too stout to be elvish. She didn't look weighty, but rather that her shoulders were more broad and her back stronger than most elvish women. *How did she get here? I wish I knew what she's thinking, what she's planning.*

Finally, he stepped to her and offered her a blanket. She looked up at him, a bit surprised, and took it.

"I can pay my passage." She didn't look up. "At the first village, I'll get off the barge and return to Twynne Rivers."

"Sure. There's a small dock at a town just on the other side of the forest. We'll be there by late tomorrow." He hesitated. "I'm Granthurg. Who are you?"

She looked up. "My name is Karendle." She said nothing more.

Granthurg nodded. He moved to a trunk by the side of the platform, and drew out bread, cheese, and a jug of ale. He offered her some, but she looked uncertain as to how to respond to his gesture.

"Go ahead," he said, and offered again. This time she took a loaf and some cheese and began to eat. He moved to the others and offered to them as well. Finally, he took his own bread back to the platform and stood by the rudder. "You were quite a surprise. I appreciate your help in the fight, but I'm not sure what you're doing with us. How did you come to be on my barge?"

She didn't seem to be too sure how to answer. After a moment, she said, "I guess I'm a bounty hunter."

"And you caught your target?"

"Yeah, I suppose." Granthurg noticed DeFrantis keeping a watchful eye on her. "I'll have to take him back to the city."

Granthurg continued, "Where are you from?"

She was done with her bread, and leaned back. She broke off a piece of cheese. "Originally, I'm from the Western Mountains."

"AH! I am, too! You're part dwarf, am I right?" She ate, then nodded. "I wondered. You're a little short for a human, but you don't have elvish features! Have you been gone from the mountains long? I was hoping to get back to my city after this river run." She simply nodded, and Granthurg started talking about the mountains and his home. Before long, he glanced out over the barge and saw that Karendle, DeFrantis, and Antonerri were all lying down on the deck, wrapped in their blankets, asleep. He smiled to himself and nodded. *We'll sort everything out tomorrow.*

He took a hold of the rudder. *It will all be fine tomorrow.*

42
Thoughts

The morning sun rose, and shone on the barge. When everyone woke, Antonerri offered to steer to allow Granthurg to sleep. After a moment of instruction, Grathurg rolled out a blanket and in moments was loudly snoring.

The others opened up the stores for more bread and cheese, and sat talking and asking questions. After a few hours of sleep, Granthurg woke and joined them. The river flowed under them smoothly and evenly, and the mid-spring breeze kept them cool in the sun. Granthurg got out his maps and each made their

120

plans. Finally, they relaxed in silence as the afternoon approached.

DeFrantis:

This giant seems very knowledgeable of the things near the river. I'm not sure where to begin looking for the kids once we get to this village. I think they're somewhere in the forest, but that's a big area to cover. Maybe someone in the town knows something.

I barely know Antonerri, but he seems committed to helping. I know I shouldn't ask him to go with me, but I'll need his help. I don't know what we're up against!

The elf and the giant seemed to show concern for the children, but they have their own plans. That's kind of a shame. It would be nice to have a giant and a real wizard along! The dwarven lady is very distant. Oh, what am I saying? This is my task, why would anyone else be bothered?

Antonerri:

I am so lost. Everything I've worked for is gone. Right now, my only clear purpose is helping DeFrantis to retrieve these children. Beyond that, who knows what the Creator has for me? Who knows what the Creator has in store at all?

Maybe He's forgotten me. I've been cast aside, adrift on this river. What's around the next bend?

Thissraelle:

It was so kind of Karendle to help me fight against the sentries sent to retrieve me. I know there will be more. My father will not rest until I've been hunted and recaptured. I need to be cautious.

DeFrantis' story of the children being sold away is tragic! Her dedication to that quest is very noble. I should help them. I have been so fortunate in my own life. But if I travel with them, I may just bring more danger along.

I DID ask for adventure, didn't I?

Karendle:

I did it. I actually did it. I captured a wizard. And from the Guild, no less! That will fetch me a nice bounty. I need to get him back to the others. But, this elf girl seems to be pretty important. She seems to be connected somehow to the Guild as well, and she's a strong wizard, too! Maybe I can capture her, too, if I'm just careful. She won't go down so easy, though, and it would probably get the giant very angry.

I'll have to play this very carefully!

Granthurg:

This is all quite a big mess. What did Rinkmorr do? What were they after? It wasn't Thissraelle, like those other wizards. I wonder if it was whatever was in Rinkmorr's trunk.

I shouldn't even think of looking in there. That's his private property. I wouldn't want him going through my maps and scrolls, so I shouldn't go through his things. But whatever is in there is changing my life, putting me in danger, so I should have a right to know what I'm tangled up in, right?

Maybe I will look.

The river flowed steadily underneath them, and the oculus drove them slowly against the current. Granthurg took in a deep breath.

122

He thought, *I have no idea what's going on, do I?*

The End of Story One

Interlude

43
Placing a Dinner Order
Tonklyn

Tonklyn stood on a large balcony, jutting out from halfway up the side of a mountain. Really, to say the balcony was large was an understatement. It was easily thirty to forty feet wide, and it jutted out over the mountainside at least twenty feet in a sweeping half circle. The light glowing from the oculus at the end of his staff barely chased the dark from the balcony's edge, enhanced a bit by the moonlight. There was no ledge or railing, just a stonework masonry floor, and then a steep and fast drop down the side of the mountain. Below the balcony were crags still full of unmelted snow, spotted with trees.

Tonklyn stood a safe distance from the edge, but not against the mountainside opposite the drop off, or particularly close to the gaping open mouth of a corridor carved into that mountain. The night breeze was cold. It was the late spring, of course, but at this altitude, the air was still winter. His heavy dark brown robes and hood kept him relatively warm as he waited.

It was a clear night, with lots of stars, and an almost full moon. The view of the forest at the valley floor below him was stunning. His eyes, however, were up in the air, scanning, looking, watching.

The balcony was built just at the timber line. There were trees below, but above him only rocks and mountain, except for two other constructions, watchtowers jutting upward out of the mountain on either side of the balcony. The wind blew stronger for a moment, and he drew his hood and cloak tighter, though his breath still formed a mist in the chill before him.

He caught sight of a motion in the air far off to his right, and his eyes focused on it immediately. It swept across the sky, silhouetted before the moon. He stepped forward and stood a little taller. As the shadow turned in the air, he raised his staff and waved it from side to side. It grew larger as it drew closer, and it came quickly. It dropped down, and for a moment was out of sight.

Tonklyn could hear the heavy flapping of huge wings and felt the wind sweeping up from the trees below. Suddenly the balcony was enveloped in shadow as a massive dragon swooped up over the edge, waving its wings to both stop and steady itself. Its neck arched over and its head looked across the balcony, finally focusing on Tonklyn, whose cloak was waving fiercely in the torrent created by the wings. As the dragon's wings drew back and up for another stroke, its back legs, easily as long as Tonklyn was high, reached down and settled onto the edge of the balcony.

The muscular body was covered in skin of deep black scales with a slight tint of red reflecting on the underside. The wingstroke came, though not as hard as others, and the forelegs reached out and landed on the stone floor. The dragon leaned back on its back legs and lifted up its head. It stretched out its wings and shook them before folding them neatly across its back. It swayed its head from side to side as if to work its muscles, and finally looked at the human.

Tonklyn stepped forward and dropped to one knee, bowing deeply. "My Liege."

The dragon snorted, enveloping Tonklyn in smoke and fumes. It turned and lowered its head to slide his body into the corridor entryway. The pounding of its feet on the floor echoed through the chambers. Tonklyn scurried after it, trying to catch up to the head. He spoke hurriedly. "There is a scroll for you, a message from the High Priests of the Church of Three Lights in Twynne Rivers. Shall I get it for you?"

"Yes. But I am hungry." The dragon's voice was guttural and raspy, and it sounded as if forming the sounds of human speech didn't come naturally to its lips. "Bring me a meal, and read it to me as I feed."

"Certainly." They stepped from the corridor into a large open chamber with a high ceiling supported by pillars all around, each with a dimly glowing oculus. In the center of this space was a vast round carpet of soft furs and blankets. The dragon strode in and circled himself onto it and settled down, with his head up and alert.

"But today, I have grown tired of cattle and venison. Bring me something more delicate."

"Yes, my Liege."

"Bring me children. Human children."

"Yes, my Liege. Right away."

Story Two

The Kids Aren't Alright

Part Four

Splitting

44
Placing a Breakfast Order
DeFrantis

The bright morning sun shone through the slightly smoke-tinted windows of the lower level of the village inn. Its lower angle swept the sunbeams across the tables and floor. There was already activity in the common room, even at this hour.

"Hearye, hearyeall!" A man in a bright red jacket shouted. The pubcrier's clothing was vivid, the red cloth trimmed in light yellow piping. His hat had long white feathers sweeping toward his back. His appearance, if not his voice, cried out for everyone's attention, and everyone in the pub turned to give it to him. He lifted a scroll and began reading the day's news.

"King Hastone III, of House Twynham, may he live long, and protect us all, has issued a decree of a tax of 3 coppers for anyone traveling the roads to and from Twynne Rivers. This includes the western road that follows the Greater Wynne River, to our fair village. This tax will allow the king to provide soldiers to protect the merchant caravans and travellers along these roads."

The few people in the common room muttered their complaints and turned their faces back to their breakfasts, or to each other.

The crier continued, "This is primarily due to increased danger from brigands and wizards along the vital trading routes."

As the crier droned on, DeFrantis squinted in the sunlight and looked across the table at Thissraelle. "I don't understand why wizardry is so despised recently." Thissraelle shrugged, as DeFrantis continued, "I guess there are always those who use powers to steal or hurt others." *I guess I have, too, but I do try to only use it to protect myself. Still, I'm not really a full wizard.*

Thissraelle leaned forward. "I spent my life hidden away in the Twynne Rivers Guild Towers. All I've known is wizards and wizardry. Mages are wonderful people. I don't understand the fear, either."

The front door swung open, flooding the floor with morning sunlight. Just as quickly, the light was obscured by a tall silhouette that stepped into the doorway and ducked through. As soon as she recognized the giant, Thissraelle waved. "Granthurg! Over here!"

DeFrantis was surprised. "Didn't he stay in the inn, too?"

"He insisted on guarding the barge." She waved again. "Here we

132

are!"

Granthurg stepped over to the table and pulled out a chair. It was clearly too small for him, but it was steady enough to support his weight. "Good morning. I trust you slept well."

DeFrantis smiled. "I'm not used to beds. It was..." she paused, thinking of what to say, "...oddly restful. I'm very grateful to you both."

Granthurg nodded and looked around. "Where are the others?"

"I've not seen either of them this morning. Antonerri is still asleep, I suppose. Presumably, the bounty hunter has left to return her capture and collect her pay." DeFrantis hesitated, "She kind of scares me, honestly. I'm not quite sure what to make of her."

The innkeeper interrupted them with steaming bowls of meal and eggs, and set drinking glasses before them. He stood at the tableside for a moment, looking at them awkwardly. It suddenly occurred to Thissraelle what he was wanting, and she dug into her purse for a few silver pieces. "Does this cover the rooms and the meal?"

"Thank you, miss!"

DeFrantis hung her head.

"What's the matter?"

"I'm not used to beds, or.. kindness."

They began eating. After a moment, Thissraelle broke the

awkwardness by asking, "Will you begin your search here?"

DeFrantis nodded between bites of egg. Granturg said, "This is the village of Dirae. I heard it's named for one of its founding settlers. It's mostly farmers working the land for a few remote nobles. It's the first trading stop on the westward trip up the Greater Wynne. It's not a big city, but it might be where they brought the children. I've heard there is a dark market here, but I don't know where. They could have tried to sell the kids there. Of course, now there are brigands in the forest attacking the caravans and even the barges. They could be holding them hostage."

The two women paused in their breakfast and just stared at the Giant.

"What? I stop here in this village every time we sail up the north river. Granted, it's not very often, but still, I hear things. People talk, especially the river runners."

"I've been in dark markets before. Maybe I'll begin there." DeFrantis said as she returned to her meal. She didn't see the concerned glances between her table companions.

45
A Very Close Shave
Antonerri

Antonerri awoke disoriented. Morning light fell across his face, making it hard to see. He blinked and rolled over, then rose up on one arm. He was on a bed. A nice one, actually, padded well with what felt like a feather mattress. With real blankets.

Wait. How did I get here?

134

As he wiped his eyes with his other hand, the memories of the last few days flowed into his head. The last bed he had slept in was in the barracks of the Holy Guard, and it was made of rough straw. That seemed like a completely different world, now.

He sat up, then stood. The wizard girl had gotten them rooms at this inn. For a small town, there was one pretty fancy inn, and she had found it. "We should all get a good night's sleep!" she had said. All but the Giant. He had wanted to stay with the barge. Antonerri had offered to stay as well, but Granthurg insisted he go. The room itself was small, but nicely furnished. The rug felt good on his bare feet. There was a small table with a wash basin and soap. He rubbed his hand across his face and felt the four days of stubble.

He crossed the room again and reached for his pouch. He pulled out a dagger and unsheathed it as he walked back to the table. It was finely crafted and had a good edge. He had picked it up after the fight on the barge. It must have dropped from one of the attackers' belts. He set it on the table and poured water from a pitcher into the basin. He rinsed off his hands, and got them soapy, spreading the foam over his chin.

His hand shook a little as he raised the dagger to his neck. Memories of the accusations of the Confessor Priest flashed through his mind. *I am unworthy. I am rejected. I have nothing, and nowhere to go. It would be simple. It would be quick. The wondering would be over.*

He stood, transfixed, feeling the cold edge of the blade on his dripping throat. He took a deep breath and shifted the dagger in his fingers. He drew down, scraping away the soap and the beard.

No. Not yet. I have to help find the children, and free them. Maybe then I can find some peace, one way or another.

When he finished shaving, he dressed. He hesitated to put on his tunic, looking at the emblem of the three star lights over the left breast. Finally, having nothing else to wear, he put it on. Then, he stepped out into the hallway, looking for DeFrantis.

46
Well, Now What?
Antonerri

Antonerri stepped down the stairs into the common area of the Inn. It looked much brighter and more welcoming than it had the night before. He could see the activity of the morning picking up, and recognized a table full of his traveling companions. As he approached, he heard DeFrantis say, "I've been in dark markets before. Maybe I'll begin there."

There was an immediate awkward silence after her statement, which Antonneri broke by pulling out a chair and sitting down.

Thissraelle was quick with a smile and a greeting, "Good Morning! How did you sleep?"

The sleeping was fine. The trouble was waking up. "Fine, thanks." He looked over the breakfast food. "Much better than in a jail cell or even an army barracks."

I'll try and keep it cordial. No need to bother them with my own struggles.

"Are you hungry? Have some!"

He nodded. He was quite hungry, and so he reached for a plate and the serving bowl. He glanced over at DeFrantis, who returned his look in a glance with a slight smile. He nodded a quiet morning greeting. As he began eating, he thought about the interesting collection of souls gathered around the table, from so many different backgrounds and experiences. As they had been traveling the day before, they had talked and, to a certain extent, gotten to know each other. He thought it odd that they would all be together at the same table. Just a few days before, none of them had known any of the others.

Oh! I'm being ungrateful! He suddenly dropped his fork and said, "Forgive me and my bad manners. A thanks to whoever provided this meal, and the bed for the night."

Thissraelle had a mouthful of food, but gestured with her hands as if to say not to worry.

"So, what was this about the dark market?" He asked, hoping to restart the discussion.

Granthurg answered, "This village has one, but I'm not sure we should get messed in with it. It's probably dangerous, and, considering how we were run out of Twynne Rivers, it might not be a good idea to be seen here among those who connect that way."

DeFrantis swallowed her spoonful. "True, but since we're already in danger, that wouldn't really make much difference, would it? We really should go where it happens. I mean, children aren't going to be sold in the open square."

Thissraelle wondered, "Doesn't the Church of Three Lights take care of orphans and street kids? Maybe we should ask the local

Priest what he might know..." Antonneri and DeFrantis both stopped eating and shared a fearful glance. Antonneri had to shake his head to resume breathing.

DeFrantis finally spoke. "This is my task. These are like my children. I should have protected them. I have to save them now. I can't require any of you to join me in this danger. Each of you have things you need to do. Thissraelle, you're wanting to go to Emberfire. That's a long Journey. Granthurg, you're needing to get the barge upriver. Antonerri..." Here she paused, then continued, "You all don't need more risk and distractions from me."

No one spoke. No one ate. For a moment, the air was decorated with the sounds of glasses clinking, footsteps, and voices mumbling from other tables. Outside, a voice and a laugh drifted through the window. Antonerri saw the elf and the giant looking at each other with questioning glances.

Granthurg cleared his throat. "Well, that's true enough. We all have our own plans. We don't have reason to get involved. Except that there are children's lives at risk." He saw Thissraelle smiling at him. "So, I think we can postpone our journeys and help."

She nodded enthusiastically. "Yes! We can!"

DeFrantis sighed with relief. "Okay, then. We're a team."

Antonerri nodded his assent, then asked, "So. What do we do first?"

47
What's in a Name? Part I
Karendle

Karendle had gotten up very early, as the dawn was first making its light in the eastern sky. She cleaned herself and dressed, then stepped out into the inn's common room. The elf girl had bought a room for everyone the night before, when they'd arrived. *What was her name? Thizarell? Tissarill?* She couldn't remember.

The innkeeper wasn't up yet, even. The hall was oddly quiet, considering how noisy and smokey it had been the previous night. She stepped through the main door and out into the street. The inn was on the waterfront, and across the street were docks. She could see the giant's barge docked several berths away to the left. The giant had insisted on staying with it.

She quietly stepped eastward, walking along the river. It flowed calmly past her, moving west toward the swamps of Umbramoor. That's where the rest of them said they were going, after they got the thing with the kids sorted out. A part of her hoped they would succeed. They seemed like sincere sort of people. Unfortunately, the kind of people that this world would chew up and spit out like bad gruel.

She had other plans.

She felt her pouch bounce against her hip as she walked. In it were the oculi, the gems she carried to give her magic. One of them, of polished granite, contained a wizard, magically trapped in the stone. She had to get this stone back to Twynne Rivers, to deliver this bounty to her contact.

So, first, I have to find a barge to take me back downstream. Actually, first I ought to contact my... My contact... Had she forgotten their names, too? No, she realized that they hadn't given her their names. In her excitement to get the oculi, and to get access to the powers they brought, she had never thought to ask, *and it's odd that they never offered their names, either.*

She took a moment and sat down on a bench by the docks. There was a slow breeze blowing with the river. It was chilly in the morning, even though the weather was warming with the summer coming on.

Where would be a good spot to reach out? They told me to do it in secret, where no one was watching...

She didn't notice, however, that someone was watching. Someone hiding across the street, by the still closed waterfront shops.

48
What's in a Name? Part II
Karendle

Karendle wrapped her cloak more tightly around her, against the chill of the morning, while she sat on the bench. She grabbed her pouch and opened it up. *They said the blue one would be for communication, and that I should only use it if I caught a wizard. I did that.* Still, she felt a bit nervous. She wasn't sure how it worked.

In the early morning shadows, she stepped toward the docks, toward some crates stacked close together. She looked for a spot that would give her a little cover. She wriggled herself in between a couple of the crates, and reached into the pouch. The first draw brought out the red gem, but the second fetched the blue. She held it in her hands and focused her concentration on it.

140

It did nothing but feel cold and smooth in her hands.

She frowned, and furrowed her brows more, as she closed her eyes and concentrated more.

Still, it did nothing.

She let out a sigh of exasperation, and held back the temptation to step out and fling the stone into the river. Instead, she just held it, and looked at it in frustration. *How do you make this thing work? The flame one and the capture one worked just fine!*

She turned it in her hand, looking at the facets carved into the sapphire. She looked at the angles, as they seemed to sparkle in the dim light. The blue hue grew deeper as she stared into it, and suddenly she realized the glimmer wasn't a reflection, but a light shining from within the stone. It became lighter and brighter as her eyes grew wider with excitement.

"What's going on?" She was startled by the voice and lurched to hide the glowing stone. She looked out beyond the crates and saw no one near. *Was that voice in my head?*

"Yes, it is." It was a man's voice, sounding very clear, as if it were close to her, but she knew she wasn't hearing it.

Uh... Hello?

"You have my attention. I'm awake. It's early, so I'm hoping you're telling me good news."

She smiled, proud to be able to deliver just that. *Yes! I caught one! I was trailing one who had tried to steal a chicken, and I caught another one instead. He's actually one of the wizard's guild.*

141

"Oh! Well. That's an interesting twist." There was a pause, and in the silence, she wondered if the communication was still flowing. She looked at the stone. It was glowing. *"How did you find him?"*

Oh, it was easy, actually. He and his friend were trying to catch another mage that was also on the barge! They said something about trying to take her home. For some reason they were all in trouble and had to sail out of town fast. I don't know what was going on, but I travelled with them to this small town upriver. I'm going to get passage back to Twynne Rivers and bring you this guy right away.

"Ok. That's a good plan. When you get here, contact us again."

"Thissraelle!" Karendle called out, as she suddenly remembered the name. Then, just as suddenly, she huddled back against the crates to hide.

"What?"

Thissraelle. That was the name of the wizard that the one I caught was chasing. I traveled upriver with her and the others.

"What? Did you say her name was Thissraelle? Is she an elf, by any chance?"

Yes. Do you know her?

"Are you still with her?"

No, she's back at the inn with the others.

The man's voice took on a new intensity, almost an excitement. *"Here's a change in your plans: Follow her. Capture her. She is your next target."*

142

Karendle was taken aback for a moment. *OK, sure! She must be pretty important, then, right?*

"You don't need to worry about that. Just bring her in with the other one, and we'll pay you well. Very well."

Sure. I'll do that. No problem. With that, the glow dimmed. She sat for a moment, thinking about Thissraelle, and wondering why she would be so critical to capture. Finally, she shrugged and stepped away from the crates, walking briskly back toward the inn.

She swore quietly under her breath. *I STILL forgot to ask them their names!*

49
Quick With the Fingers
Karendle

Karendle stepped away from the crates and shook herself off. The light was starting to show a bit more in the eastern sky. She looked up and down the street to check if anyone had seen her. Across the street were some shops, and someone was there with a large cart, beginning to unload things onto the street in front. There was nobody the other way. *It looks like it's clear.*

The chilly breeze blew past her as she began walking westward, back toward the inn. She picked up her pace, a bit excited.

If I can get back before everyone gets up, I could even sneak into her room and take her from there. Then, it would be easy to slip away, get on a barge or a caravan heading east, and be gone!

She was so wrapped up in thought that she didn't see the figure step up at her side, or the stick swing across her path and her shins, sending her face-first onto the cobblestones. The pain shot harshly through her legs. She tried to roll over but suddenly felt a weight land on her. Someone had jumped onto her back, and was pressing her face into the street. She twisted and squirmed, trying to get a hand hold to press herself up.

"Hold still, wench!" He leaned a knee between the shoulder blades and pulled back her cloak. "There it is. I knew when you came out of that nice inn, you'd have some money!" She felt a harsh tug and a snap at her belt and suddenly the weight and pressure on top of her were gone. She heard his footsteps rush down the street. She rolled and saw him running east. He dashed quickly between a couple of buildings.

She tried to stand, but the pain in her shin bones racked her legs and she sank back to her knees. She glanced at her hips. *He got my pouch! My oculi! My bounty!*

Wincing through the pain, she stood and lurched toward the alley where he had gone. Gradually she picked up speed and was able to start walking, then running.

When she got to the alley, she turned and a short breeze blew a noxious odor of manure and trash past her. In the dark she could see piles of rubble. Looking deeper, she saw light ahead, probably another street.

She swore, a little more loudly, and stumbled in.

144

The morning sun in the eastern sky cast shadows before DeFrantis and Antonerri as they walked along the waterfront. Shops and taverns were beginning to open up, and dockworkers were unloading barges. Others, who just brought wares to sell, were laying out baskets of grain or fruits onto rugs and blankets on the side of the street. She had never been to Dirae before. It was not a large city, like Twynne Rivers, or even Portstown. But whereas most villages were little more than a collection of a few hovels where farmers and peasants gathered at the end of the work day, this one had streets of cobblestone, a series of docks on the river, and buildings and businesses.

The streets along the river were pretty clean, too, but walking past the side streets, DeFrantis could see that the paving ended quickly, and the mess and mud quickly replaced it.

Antonerri finally spoke, "So where would we find this dark market?"

"In Twynne Rivers, the dark market isn't a place. It's more of a network. It's a lot harder to shut down that way. Where you go depends on what you're wanting to find."

He nodded. "...Or what you're wanting to sell."

"Yes. So, once we find a hub, they might be able to direct us to the right place."

"Once, while I was a guard, our unit was sent to break up one such hub. We just went where we were told and arrested them."

145

DeFrantis laughed. "It was probably another dark marketer who sent you. They must have had an argument over a payment or something. You were just doing the cleanup!" She nudged his arm and smiled.

He laughed, too, but not as enthusiastically. "So, what should we be looking for? Do we want to act like we're buying something?"

She thought a moment, and stopped walking. She looked around at the shops. "No, I think we'll be sellers. But we'll have to get you some nicer clothes. And with something other than the Church's seal. It's a good thing you shaved. The half-beard wouldn't have worked."

"Worked for what?" He was genuinely confused. "What will we say we're selling?"

"You, my friend," She said, "Will be selling me."

51
Going to the Chapel
Thissraelle

"Maybe I'm too naive." Thissraelle admitted. "It's true that I barely know these people. And we're being hunted by the Wizard's Guild and who knows who else..."

She and Granthurg walked along the waterfront, to the west, as the road followed the flow of the river. The morning busy-ness of the markets was beginning to show on the street. The shops were opening, and vendors were setting up by the side of the road. The sun rising over the town's houses had replaced quiet with chatter. The barmaid at the inn had told her that following this road would take them to the town's small cathedral.

146

She continued, "But then, I barely know you, too. And I find you to be trustworthy."

He smiled. "Thank you. DeFrantis and her friend seem to be sincere enough, I guess. I'm just wary."

"That's probably a good thing, I would think." She glanced up, and pointed over a shop's roof. "I'll bet that spire ahead is the chapel." He nodded.

They stepped over someone's basket of grain. "You seem to be lost in thought. What's worrying you? Besides what we've already talked about, I mean."

"I'm wondering," He said, looking at the spire she had pointed out. Not really at it so much as beyond it. "What is on our barge that made those men attack us back in the city? What is it they want?"

She shrugged and looked behind her for a moment. "I'm wondering something, too." Then she looked west again, down the street. "Where are the children? Twynne Rivers had lots of them, running in the streets, playing, begging, stealing. There are none here."

They passed the building before them and then stood in front of the cathedral. It was tall, but not as expansive and majestic as the one in the Twynne Rivers Center Towne. This one was plain stone, with smaller, circular stained glass for windows along the sides. It had no lawn, no foliage. It opened simply onto the street. There was a tall spire with a bell tower pointing upward to heaven, and a single larger stained window below it, depicting three bright yellow stars. *The Church of Three Lights. I wonder why Antonerri and DeFrantis were so insistent on not coming here. His shirt bears that same image. You'd think that he'd want to talk with them.*

Granthurg turned his eyes away from the chapel to look at Thissraelle. "Well, let's hope they know where they've all gone."

52
Brother, Sister, Friends
Granthurg

Granthurg pushed on the large wooden door. It gave way easily, though not without a sound. As it creaked, he stepped inside and looked at the cathedral hall before him. Immediately the vaulted ceiling and the arches supporting it surrounded him with a sense of smallness. The hall itself wasn't so much big as its openness and vastness made him feel small. The colored lights of the morning streaming in through the windows covered the benches in warmth, but left the upper lofts shrouded in shadow and smoke from candles, incense, and hearthfires.

There was a peace, a calm about this place that he found oddly familiar, and, as he looked across the room, made him smile. Churches had always made him feel a bit uneasy, like he was unworthy of being there. But today, it reminded him of an easy summer night on the river, and it filled him with relaxation. He felt an urge to kneel, but he didn't know where, so he simply stood, awkwardly, in silence, as Thissraelle moved out from behind him.

She stepped forward, interrupting his reverie, toward a man who had been walking up the aisle toward them. Granthurg had been so enraptured by the building that he had ignored the man entirely. He was a human, but a bit short, and plump. He wore the robes of a monk, not a priest. His hair was cropped short, and

148

his beard was trimmed. He bowed as he approached.

"Welcome! Welcome! A fair day to you both!" Thissraelle extended her hand in greeting. He took it, then surprised her by drawing her into an enthusiastic hug. He set her back down and reached up to Granthurg, who backed away slightly. *I don't know about this...*

"Oh, come here!" The brother gently chided, and moved closer to Granthurg, reaching up to embrace the giant. He hesitated, then found himself relaxing. He received and returned the hug. After a couple of gentle pats on the back, the old friar released him and stepped back. "I'm so glad to see you both! Come! Come up here and sit down!"

Granthurg found himself chuckling at his odd and overly friendly style, and followed him toward the altar before the pews. Thissraelle also followed.

"I'm Brother Mathazar. We don't get many visitors," He gestured to the benches, then sat himself on the edge of the altar's dias, "Especially mid-day, and mid-week."

Thissraelle sat on the most forward bench, and Granthurg eased himself down next to her. The bench groaned under his weight, but held.

"What brings you here, today," Brother Mathazar said, "Confession? Worship service? Marriage?"

Thissraelle coughed, startled. "Oh, no! No! We're here because we need your help. One of our traveling companions is looking for some missing children. We believe they might have been brought through this town."

The sudden silence in the thick air was palpable. Brother Mathazar looked closely at each of them. "That would mean you're not from around here. That would mean you don't know about Dirae, do you?"

Granthurg's eyes narrowed. "I've been through here before. I work the river. Mostly the Lesser Wynne, though."

"When was the last time you came by here?"

Granthurg thought about this. *How long ago was it? I was working the Portstown runs last year, and I wintered at home in the mountains.* "Perhaps two, maybe three summers ago..."

"About a year ago, Dirae became a dark market hub. One of the darkest kind. There, they buy and sell the saddest of wares." He got very quiet. "They're slavers!"

He saw their reactions, and continued, "They'll sell anyone, from anywhere! Even children! They have no shame! And they're ruthless and bloody. They'll kill anyone that gets in the way."

Thissraelle ventured, "Is that why we see no children begging in the streets here?"

"Yes!" the brother whispered, "Good parents won't let their kids out of their sight, and kids without get snatched up and sold! We had to move our orphanage to the abbey in the forest to keep them safe! The people have gone crazy, here. Every once in a while, there's a big fight in the streets as rival guilds vie for control. Outside of the waterfront, people just work their farms and stay inside. They don't come to church any more. Most of them are too afraid."

150

Granthurg saw Thissraelle's head droop. His large hand rested on her narrow shoulder. She looked up and said, "When will I stop being amazed by the horrors I see?"

"Oh, my dear sister," sighed Brother Mathazar, "My dear, dear sister..."

53
Stopping a Thief, Part I
Karendle

Karendle tried to run through the alley, but it was too cluttered and her knee and shin were painful and weak. The best she could do in the shadows of the dim morning light was to limp and stumble her way forward. After a few yards, she saw some barrels stacked along the side of the building and reached out to them for support. Her eyes adjusted. *Maybe it's just getting lighter.* She steadied herself and ran ahead.

I can't lose him! He had to come this way!

She came to a spot that was a bit lighter, where the alley intersected with another at the end of the building, along a fence. *Which way to go?* She looked each way. *I'll bet he went left,* she told herself, and took off that way.

Immediately, her foot hit some garbage and she tripped. She fell, hard, onto the dirt of the alley. Just as quickly she heard something shout in pain. *That wasn't me.*

She flipped over and leaned up. Next to a couple of crates was a small, brown burlap tarp. The broken twine at the corners suggested that it had probably been covering the crates at one point. Something was moving under the clutter. *Yes, there are two legs sticking out from under that wrap!.* Ignoring the sharp pain in her leg, she stood and whisked the tarp away.

"No! Don't take me! Don't take me! Let me go home!" He was thin, and looked a bit old. The empty jug on his arm and the ale-soaked shirt told her his story.

"Hey!" She said, grabbing him and picking him up. She leaned him against the wall.

"Don't take me!" He shrieked again. She winced at the toxic smell of alcohol that wafted from him. His tunic was also a dull brown and caked with dirt and dust.

"I'm not taking you anywhere!" She shouted, shaking him. "Who would want you?" She let go and he slumped down again, mumbling. *Wait. He might have seen the thief.*

"I'll go home..."

"Did someone just run by here?"

He looked up at her, confused.

"I"m not going to hurt you! Just tell me if someone came through here!"

He sighed and wiped his face as he cleared his thoughts. Then, he nodded, and pointed. "Yeah. Just now. Did you get robbed?"

"Yeah." She limped off in that same direction. *Yeah. I got robbed.*

He called after her. "Watch out! Don't let them take you!"

Karendle didn't allow herself a moment to wonder what he meant.

Part Five

Separation

54
Stopping a Thief, Part II
Karendle

I've lost him. I've lost the thief, lost the wizard, lost it all.

The sun was much brighter, shining down in mid-morning glory, and making the market air warm. Karendle wasn't feeling it. She had just spent the last hours limping up and down the alleyways of this little town's center. Back and forth, over and over, looking for some sign of the man in the dark cloak that had robbed her. By now, her leg was hurting her less, or maybe she was just getting used to it.

This is a small town! There isn't that much to see! Where could he be hiding? She looked up and down the street. There were vendors lining the far side of the street, away from the docks, mostly squatting on blankets with grains or cloth spread out before them. The de facto marketplace only went for a few blocks either way. She had asked a few of the vendors, but no one had seen the man she described.

The street was getting more full as the sun kept rising. Karendle found a bench near some bushes where she could rest and rub out the pain in her leg. *I'm sure that by now, he's opened the pouch up and tried to sell the oculi. Is there a jeweler in this town? Maybe he knows they're magical. He can probably get some good money out of oculus stones.*

The sun was getting warm on the side of her face. *Of course, stones like that would have to be sold in a dark market. There's no way anyone would have those out in the open. I wonder if there's a dark market jeweler?*

She sat up and raised her head. Something familiar caught her eye. It was DeFrantis stepping out of a shop onto the main road, not more than ten yards away! A man was following her. It was Antonneri, but he was dressed differently. His church tunic was gone, and replaced by a finer shirt. His five-day beard was gone, too, and she was suddenly struck by how handsome he looked. *I'll bet DeFrantis thinks so, too!* That thought made her smile.

Quickly, she jumped up and stepped behind the bushes near the water. She leaned and watched them closely. *What are they doing? Shopping? I thought they were going to go find some kids they were looking for.* They talked to each other, but she was too far away to hear. They looked too focused, intent, to be casually shopping. They walked eastward down the street, into the sunlight.

She watched them go, wondering, then came out from the

156

bushes. *All that time I spent chasing her, and now, here I am, without my oculus to catch her. They could probably lead me back to Thissarill, too.*

Her mind was racing. So many things. *How can I find my gems? How can I find a secret, dark market? Where would I look?*

Her mind drifted, then suddenly focused on the memory of the man behind the building. *Wait! I'll bet he knows! I'll bet he's seen a lot more than he lets on! He'll know where to look!*

With an unsteady gait, she took off to find the alley.

55
What's She Worth?
DeFrantis

"I don't like this!" Antonerri whispered.

"I know. But you look very good like that." DeFrantis stood in front of her friend, with her back to him.

"I wasn't talking about the shirt." The room was dark, even though it was day. The windows of the old inn had been boarded up. Only a few thin rays of light shone through the cracks. It was also crowded, with people pressing their way in, out, and around the cramped space. There was a low rumble of voices filling the warm, smoky, damp air.

"I know you weren't. We'll be fine," DeFrantis said. Her hands were tied in front of her, not too tightly, but enough to show who was the seller and who was for sale. Antonerri held onto the other end of that short rope like a child held his mother's hand. She continued, "You shouldn't be talking to me. Push me around a bit. Find a buyer."

He half-heartedly nudged her forward and she took a few steps, angling between a few others. She added, "And keep an eye out for children."

"Quiet, you!" He nudged her again, then whispered, "Sorry". She tried not to laugh. They stepped cautiously through the crowd.

To her left, two men spoke quickly to each other, gesturing intensely with their hands. One of them had a hold on a chain attached to two other younger men. They were in tattered tunics, and their thin, frail bodies were covered in mud and dirt. Their eyes were down, and hidden by scraggly strands of hair. Their slightly elongated ears told her they were wood elves. *Probably from Umbrawood forest. I wonder if they came to Dirae on their own or if the slavers had taken them in a raid on their treehold.*

The two humans shook hands. As DeFrantis and Antonerri continued moving, she saw one give the other a pouch. Then they were lost from sight in the press. *We have to shut this down. So much suffering. But not yet. I have to stay focused.*

She felt Antonerri stop and turn when someone with a deep, gruff voice said, "Let me see her!" A hand grabbed her shoulder and spun her around. Instinctively, her hand reached up to block, but she immediately realized it was tied to her other hand, and it reminded her not to react. She kept her gaze down.

The man standing in front of her wore tall boots of fine leather. His leggings and shirt were clean, and appeared to be expensive linen. He reached his hand up and grabbed her jaws and cheeks, then pulled her face upward and looked her over. His face was shadowed, but human and angular, bent in a scowl. With a look

158

of disdain and a harsh shove on her cheek, the buyer turned back to Antonerri.

"I'll give you two gold," the buyer rasped, "And that's generous." He pushed her head down again.

She threw a worried glance at Antonerri and saw his jaw tense. Quickly, nervously, she dropped her head again, like the obedient captive she was supposed to be.

This could get ugly really fast.

56
A walk in the Countryside
Granthurg

Granthurg and Thissraelle left the chapel and walked in silence. It was just before mid-day, so the streets were very busy with townspeople going about their business. In spite of the noise around them, they said nothing to each other.

Their original plan had been for each group to find out what they could and to reconvene at the inn for further planning. Somehow, Granthurg felt an urgency to go where Brother Mathazar had directed them. In a hushed voice, the acolyte had said, "Keep following the main road west, along the river. You'll leave the town. Soon, you'll find a way that turns off to the north and leads to a few buildings. One of those buildings used to be a waypoint inn. It's the dark market, now."

Brother Mathazar had continued, "But be cautious, and ready. If you're attacked and defeated, you'll be taken and sold. I daresay, you'd both get a pretty hefty price. You, for your strength." He had motioned to Granthurg, then to Thissraelle, "And you, for, well... Other things."

After the quiet pause that followed, he'd added, "You're both very selfless and brave for helping your friends. I wish you the very best!"

It wasn't long before the buildings became groves, meadows, and farmlands. They had been plowed and sown, but the crops were only beginning to appear above the ground. Keeping the unwanted weeds away was a constant task, and there were farmers and vassals out in the fields striking at them with hoes and digging them with sticks.

They were less than a mile from the edge of the town when they saw the small cluster of buildings around a larger, central structure. There were lots of wagons and horses tied to posts and fences around the perimeter.

"Hmph." Granthurg grunted, "For such a remote place, there are a lot of people."

Thissraelle nodded, "We probably shouldn't approach from the road."

"Good point." He looked around. "How about that knoll with the hedges on the far side?"

"We can keep walking on the road as if we're passing onward, and then double back." She drew her cloak around her, in spite of the noonday sun. A wagon started leave the compound, its driver steering the team along the narrow, but well-worn path to the main road. They picked up their pace a bit so they wouldn't cross their paths.

Another man had been walking along behind them. He carried a bulging pack over his shoulder, filled with a bundle of sticks.

Granthurg glanced down at Thisraelle and turned his gaze back to the road.

57
I See Them!
DeFrantis

The moment hung heavily in the air. DeFrantis stood, frozen, in front of Antonerri, and looking at the fancy shoes of a possible buyer, a human she didn't know. She waited, her arms tense, gently flexing her wrists. They were tied, but only lightly. She could scrunch her hands together and slip them out of the ropes very easily; they were only there for show. The tall human had made an offer, and Antonerri was silent.

What's he thinking? I hope he's playing this like he's considering the offer. He's probably scared to death. He doesn't have a lot of practice playing a slaver. Maybe he can work that to his advantage.

Antonerri cleared his throat and finally spoke. "Hmmm. Two gold is a lot. I could buy a lot with two gold."

No! You're not supposed to actually sell me!

"But I have to split any coin I get with her father. I'll have to go at least four." She heard Antonerri's voice, trying to sound resolute. "At least four gold pieces."

The other man laughed. "You'll not get even two from anyone but me! Look at her!" DeFrantis began to glance from side to side, always keeping her head down, trying to figure out what was happening around her. She vaguely heard Antonerri's voice responding. As she looked to her right, through the forest of legs and torsos, she thought she saw a small person's bare foot.

He head snapped to her right and her eyes focused, shifting forward and back to see through the people. *Yes! There they are!* She could clearly see two children - no, three - huddled close together. They were dressed in dirty, ill-fitting tunics and without shoes. Her body tensed as chills shivered through her. *They look so lost! I have to save them! Wait! No. I have to follow them. I have to find who's buying them and where they're being taken -*

She looked up at Antonerri, but his attention was on the buyer's face. They were deep in negotiations, but the thoughts in her head blocked out any words she was hearing. She moved her head in the direction of the children to try and get his attention. It wasn't working. She looked back at the children, but like a spider on the floor, they were gone.

Wait! Where did they go? I only looked away! Where are they? She leaned her body to get a better look at where they were, but other captives and sellers had moved in her way. She lifted up on her toes and craned her neck, but she was not very tall in the first place, and couldn't see over the press of people. She suddenly heard the buyer's voice cut through.

"Hey, where are you going?" DeFrantis looked at him, then at Antonerri and suddenly realized she had slipped several feet away, and the rope was tugging at her hands. "You'd better keep your maid in line!" Antonerri was stunned, not sure what to do.

DeFrantis immediately went back to her demure role, but glanced up and used her head to point to where she saw the children. *Please, just look over there! Help me find them!*

162

A loud crash and shouts from the other side of the room interrupted the hesitation of the instant. Everyone's head turned. Sellers and buyers alike were shouting and falling away from what looked like a fight. Someone bumped into DeFrantis and knocked her over. Immediately, she shouted and moved her hands to shelter her face from the rushing feet around her. The rope seemed loose, so she started working her hands free. She rolled over and tried to get up on her knees, but it was difficult with tied hands.

"Antonerri!" She called out, but his voice was lost in the noise.

My hands are free! Now it was easy for her to lean forward and stand. Her street instincts reminded her to stay fairly low, for a more solid balance. She looked left, and right, searching for both the children and Antonerri.

A loud and bright explosion instantly lit the small room and knocked everyone off their feet, either struck by it's force or ducking for cover. The concussion left DeFrantis stunned. As the ringing in her ears subsided, she sat up and shook her head, crawling away from where the explosion had happened.

She started to make

out actual voices, mostly shouting things like, "Wizards!" and "Run!" She saw people begin to flood away from the room looking for exits wherever they could. As she crawled and struggled to stand, she saw a familiar face, contorted in pain, lying on the floor.

"Karendle? What... ?" Her voice trailed off as she saw the dagger and the blood.

58
I've Heard that Boom Before!
DeFrantis

"Karendle!" DeFrantis began crawling and shuffling her way over. She shielded her head and face with her free hand as dozens of feet ran around her head. The flurry of motion made her dizzy for a moment, her head still ringing from the explosion.

What happened? I was with Antonerri and there was a blast. What happened here, to Karendle? DeFrantis reached out and grabbed Karendle's hand, pulling herself closer.

Antonerri. Where's Antonerri? I was looking for the children. Is he looking for the children? She tried to stand, to look through the scattering crowd, but dizziness brought her back down.

She raised her head and looked at Karendle, who lay partly on her side, partly on her chest. Her head was up, straining to see DeFrantis. Blood was all over the dwarf's shirt, all over the floor. *You're hurt. You're badly hurt.* Karendle's eyes were full of fear and pain. Her right hand reached out toward DeFrantis, and with her left, tried to support herself while clutching a small pouch.

There was an explosion. Where's Antonerri? Is he OK? There was an

164

explosion. There was a sudden moment of clarity in her mind. *There was an explosion. I've heard that explosion before. I've seen it. Someone threw that explosion at us when we were escaping the guard tower. I'll never forget it. Someone tried to kill us, then chased after us.*

DeFrantis drew back and looked down at Karendle. Memories filled her head. It was only a few nights ago, but it felt like forever. "That was you!" DeFrantis gasped and backed away. "That was you hunting after us!".

Karendle's mouth moved as if she was trying to speak. Her bloody hand reached up to DeFrantis.

So why didn't you attack us on the barge? Why did you help defend us? She rose up again, just to her knees this time, and looked around. Much of the room had cleared, but there were still some people scrambling for the few exits.

Where is Antonerri? Where are the children? What are we doing? She looked back down at Karendle, into her pleading eyes.

I can't let her die! With a sigh, she scurried over and turned her more on her side. The dagger was stuck in Karendle's ribcage, under her left arm. Karendle coughed twice, forcefully, and DeFrantis settled her back down.

What can I do? I've used shadows to take away hurt and pain, and heal little scrapes the kids had, but never anything like this! She took a deep breath and put her hand on Karendle's shoulder. Karendle turned her head and looked up at DeFrantis. She took hold of the dagger, let out her breath, and pulled it out. Karendle shrieked in pain, and jerked. Blood flowed fresh out of the wound over her already-stained shirt. DeFrantis immediately covered the wound with her hands and focused her concentration. The room was already dark, but a darker mist swirled up over her, around her, and over Karendle.

Karendle coughed and her body jerked. DeFrantis heard her cough again, then again. Finally, Karendle sucked in a deep breath, and rolled over onto DeFrantis' legs, then continued to rasp and wheeze all of the blood and fluid out of her lungs.

The darkness subsided and DeFrantis dropped her head to Karendle's shaking shoulder.

59
Children in the Chaos
Antonerri

The explosion shook Antonerri to the floor. His head was dazed, but he struggled back to his feet. Others were also standing up. He tried to hold his head to steady the room, but it didn't seem to help. *DeFrantis! Where is DeFrantis?*

He turned to look where he thought she had been. Instead he saw the angry face of the buyer he had been negotiating with. The man was shouting at him, but Antonerri couldn't hear the words he was saying over the ringing in his ears. The ringing was clearing, and he was starting to make out sounds. He looked at the buyer, confused, as the man drew back and punched Antonerri full in the face, knocking him back, stunned, onto the floor.

Feet were flying all around him. He rolled over, partly to stand, but mostly to protect himself in the stampede of people fleeing the market. He was hearing, now, and people were shouting and fighting.

"Wizards! Run!"

"It's the city guard!"

"Hide!"

Antonerri scrambled to get up, but a knee in his back knocked him down again. A second try got him up on one knee. "DeFrantis!" He called out, as he frantically scanned the room. All he could see was a flurry of bodies. All he could hear were shouts and crashes.

As he turned his head, he saw a man carrying two very young children, one under each arm. Ahead of him, he pushed a third, slightly older child toward a door. The children were screaming and covering their faces with hands that were tied together, and tied to each other. This made it tricky for the one on foot to keep moving, and Antonerri saw the slaver shouting and pushing the stumbling child forward.

Children! Antonerri lunged ahead. *DeFrantis wanted to find children! She'll be chasing the children!* He pushed through the crowd trying to get to the man. In a moment Antonerri was where he had been standing, but the slaver had moved on. People were pressing out the door and running. Antonerri followed, rushing through.

The bright lights of the noonday sun hit his face and people behind him pushed him out. He stumbled, and caught his balance on a barrell. People were rushing to horses and wagons. Some of the wagons and carriages were finely made, others were old and worn. They hurried to get them loaded and ready. Many were fighting with each other, shouting about who owned which slave.

Antonerri stumbled forward, then ran between some wagons. He recognized some of them as having the livery and heraldry of a few of the noble houses of Twynne Rivers. They began rolling away as he came through them, making him jump back to avoid being run over.

He stepped into the clear and scanned the scene, as people mounted up and fled. *There they are!*

The slaver was roughly handing the children up into a wagon, to another man, who grabbed them, one at a time, and threw them down inside. Antonerri rushed forward.

He threw himself at the slaver behind the wagon, knocking him to the ground. They rolled, struggling and wrestling, away from the wagon. Antonerri landed on top, and managed to land a good punch to the man's chest. Antonerri felt a painful hit from behind and was knocked to the ground. Suddenly, someone else was on top of him, driving a knee into his guts, and pummeling him with fists to his shoulders and face.

Where's DeFrantis? Then his mind went black.

60
...With the Greatest of Ease
Thissraelle

Once they had gotten a good distance past the road that turned off to the north, toward the buildings, Granthurg stepped off the road into the meadow. Thissraelle followed. They walked, casually, north, but slightly away from the old inn compound. They were trying not to draw attention to themselves.

Thissraelle looked up at Granthurg. *I am very lucky to have found a friend like this out in this world. Still, I hardly know him.* She looked back down at the meadow at her feet. *With all the craziness that I've seen since I left the tower just a few days ago, I am amazed to be still alive.*

My father tried to trap me, there, but he also taught me well. The powers of light and the dimensions have served me.

They walked down the backslope of a low hill, and began to turn their path back toward the buildings, toward the hedgerows on the knoll. Granthurg was taller, of course, and was looking back over the hill crest.

But even with that, I feel much safer when I'm near him. Not just safe from danger, either. She looked ahead across the field. *I'm not sure if he'll want to go with me all the way to Emberfire, though.*

Granthurg interrupted her thoughts with a harsh whisper. "The man with the bundle of sticks is following us."

"What?" She started up the slope to get a look.

Granthurg stepped before her and crouched. He gestured to her to stay down as well. "He turned down the road to the inn, then stepped off into the meadows. I can't see him, now."

"Let's hurry," he said, and began a low squat run behind the hills to the hedges. Once there, they crawled up to the crest to look between the branches of the bushes. They were actually fairly close to the buildings, maybe only a few dozen yards. The buildings themselves were old and falling apart. There were no windows, just spaces with wooden planks covering the way. There were many horses, carts, wagons, and carriages waiting outside the cluster. A few had people near them, waiting for someone to bring out either purchases or money from within. From the compound a rough rutted wagon trail led to the south, back to the main road.

Thissraelle spoke softly, "That's a lot of wagons. How do that many people fit in that small building?"

Granthurg grunted a muffled noise. She saw him scanning the brush and gentle hills of the meadow, looking for the man. He spoke, half to himself, "He was wearing a gray tunic and carrying a big bundle of sticks."

"Who is he after?" Thissraelle thought, apparently out loud.

"Maybe he thinks I have that thing they're looking for." Granthurg said, "Maybe they're the ones that are after you."

She looked up at him, suddenly feeling not so safe. He shrugged.

A sudden loud boom sounded from within the main hall. The walls of the building muffled it a bit, but it was still very strong, and they strained to look to see what had happened. They could make out shouts and shrieks from within the building.

"What was - " Thissraelle started to speak, but stopped when people began pouring out of the few exits in the inn. She could hear their shouts more clearly, but there were too many of them to make out any actual words.

They ran to their horses and wagons, and began to mount up and turn away down the path. Some were dragging slaves in ropes or shackles, and they were hindered and slowed by their burdens, as they were loaded up into the wagons. Other buyers and sellers

170

began fighting in the yard surrounding the buildings.

"Look!" Granthurg pointed. One slaver was running toward a well-made and well-worn wagon, a short distance from the others. It had a light-colored cover, and a crest on the on the old and weathered side. Under each arm was a young child, and he pushed another child stumbling ahead of him. "Children!"

Children? Her mind's eye flashed with images of the poverty stricken street kids of Twynne Rivers. *Children?* More memories of her own happy childhood in the guild hall. *Children?* An ugliness welled up inside her, an anger deeper than the common little arguments with her parents. She felt her body tense and her breathing quicken. The world around her started to slow.

The slaver reached the back of the wagon and began handing the kids up to someone waiting inside. The children kicked and shouted as they were roughly lifted and dragged into the wagon. As he finished, another figure in rumpled clothing rushed up behind him and tackled him to the ground.

"ANTONERRI!" Granthurg shouted. He scrambled to his feet and crashed through the hedgerow. He unslung his hammer as he started running.

Thissraelle, her eyes huge and raging, leapt up and lifted herself into the air, sailing effortlessly over Granturg and the meadow toward the wagon. She didn't even stop to realize she was flying.

171

With a shriek and a loud thud, Thissraelle landed her feet hard on the top of the wagon. The two slavers who had been fighting with Antonerri stood and looked up at her in surprise, but smirked when they saw her. Her frail high-elf body shook with tension and rage. Her head and hands burst into vivid blue light. Her white cloak, shirt, and hair flew in a magical wind swirling around her.

She pointed at one and spoke with a harsh and cutting tone, "You...,"

She floated slowly down from the wagon top to hover just above the blades of grass, which now lashed back and forth as she approached, "...Will leave...,"

She drifted toward the man who had last been fighting Antonerri, who had been in the wagon tossing the children. "...These children...,"

The man reached down to his belt, pulled out a dagger, and rushed toward Thissraelle. She stretched out her arm toward him and he froze, then rose up in the air, his arms and legs swinging wildly as he tried to grasp or kick at anything that would feel like solid ground. "Help! Help! Set me down! Set me down!" He screamed.

The other slaver ran at her from the other side, crouching low, with an angry scowl. A few steps in, and Thissraelle faced him. She raised her other arm to him, stopping him full in his tracks. As his grimace turned to fear, she swung her arm aside, like she

172

were throwing away garbage. His body followed her motion, tossed through the air, slamming into the back of the wagon hard enough to lurch the wagon forward. The children inside shrieked. The man struggled to gain control, to stand up. Another wave of her hand and she slammed him back into the wagon. Finally, he fell still and slumped to the ground.

She turned to back to the remaining slaver and drew him to her until his terrified face looked into hers. She hovered there with him struggling mere inches from her open hand. "You... will leave... the children... be!"

She surged her mind and pushed him away in disgust. The slaver flew across the meadow like a leaf in the wind, crashing across the grass and falling down a hillslope.

Thissraelle breathed in deep and fell to the ground, gasping. Her mind cleared, her body shaking, her will was drained. She looked at her hands. There was no more blue fire. She sat up and ran her fingers back through her hair, pulling it away from her face. The rage was gone.

She turned her head up and looked. There was the wagon, with the defeated slaver lying beneath it. Her eyes raised further, and saw the face of a child staring at her from the inside, with a strange mix of hope and fear.

"Oh, child!" Thissraelle stood and rushed over, reaching up and taking the child in a tight embrace. Over her shoulder, she could see two others cowering in the depths of the wagon, and she gestured to them as well. "Come! You're safe, now! You're safe!"

They scrambled over to her and she held them tight, stroking their hair. She heard the children's sobbing mixed with the distant clashing of metal on metal.

62
Fighting Over What?
Granthurg

Granthurg shouted, "ANTONERRI!" before he jumped up and broke through the bushes in the hedgerow. He unslung his hammer as he started running. The pounding of his heart in his head matched the heavy thud of his feet on the ground.

He could see Antonerri struggling with the two men at the wagon. *Hold on, there, friend! I'm on my way!*

In an instant, something swept his feet out from under him, and he fell forward, reaching out to block his fall. He hit the ground hard, and the handle of his hammer bounced and struck the side of his face. That pain was harsh, but immediately a heavy weight landed on his back and grabbed at his neck. The blow knocked Granthurg windless, and dropped him fully to the ground, pinning him there.

"You're going to sell it, aren't you?" a voice said. A sword blade appeared in Granthurg's peripheral vision. He rolled a bit to one side and brought up his arm to shield his face from the blade. The motion caught his attacker off guard for a moment. "You're going to sell it to the Dragon's Flame, aren't you? They'd love to get their hands on it!"

Won't these people ever leave me alone? Granthurg took advantage of the moment by twisting his body the other way, throwing the man off balance. He rolled away, grabbing his hammer as he did.

They both stood and faced each other. Granturg felt warm blood running down his face. Was that from the hammer or the blade? He wasn't sure, and didn't want to lose his focus on the attacker. He held his hammer before him ready to block with the handle or swing with the mass.

"Maybe you idiots would get some useful answers if you just told me what it is you're after!"

"Maybe I'll just take it from you after I kill you!"

Granthurg steeled his stance. He could hear Thissraelle's voice shouting, but couldn't make out what she was saying. *I don't have time to waste on this! She needs my help!*

"Not today, you won't!" He lunged ahead. The man was nimble and quick with the sword, but Granthurg blocked his assaults with the hammer's handle. Twice he landed hard blows with the butt end of the handle. "Does that feel good? It hurts, doesn't it?"

They danced a tight choreography of thrust, parry, hit, shift. The attacker faked a motion to the left and went in with a lunge from the right. Granthurg twisted to barely avoid the blade, which cut through his vest and shirt. The man stepped back to re-set his

175

stance. Granthurg wiped the blood from his face, then shifted the grip on his hammer.

"Didn't it ever occur to any of you," he hissed, "That if I had it, I would probably use it to defend myself?"

The man's eyes narrowed, and he rushed in, sword first, reaching in for the kill.

Granthurg shifted, and swept his hammer by the handle, parrying the incoming sword to the side. He continued to swing it up above his shoulder and back down onto his assailants extended hip, with a crackling and crunching noise. The man shrieked and collapsed onto the ground, writhing in agony.

Granthurg stood and caught his breath. "You wait here."

63
She's Just Fine
Thissraelle

"Thissraelle!" She raised her head from the crying children at the sound of Granthurg's voice. His face was wide, covered in worry, surprise, and quite a bit of blood.

"Granthurg! Are you alright?" She released the children from her embrace across the back of the wagon, and reached up to his forehead. It was cut and still drizzling blood over his eye and cheek. "You're hurt!" She turned to the wagon and began to tear a strip of cloth from the covering.

"I'm fine! Are you harmed? Where's Antonerri?"

She laughed quietly and turned to him with the torn rag. "I'm

OK!" She began wiping his face. It was cut, but not deeply. He winced as she touched it. He looked over and saw the unconscious forms scattered around. He stepped over to Antonerri, who was beginning to moan. Granthurg leaned over him. The side of his face was beginning to bruise, and his shallow breath sounded raspy.

Thissraelle said, quietly, "I can't heal him now. My powers and will are drained."

Granthurg nodded. "We need to leave. I was attacked. There could be more." Granthurg gently picked Antonerri up and lifted him into the back of the wagon. The children made room for him, and watched Granturg warily. Thissraelle climbed into the back of the wagon with them, and set some blankets under Antonerri's head. He was dressed differently than he had been earlier. He was wearing a finely made shirt, which was rumpled and roughed, even though it looked newly crafted. His scruff of a beard was gone, too, shaved off.

She looked out of the back. Granthurg was staring intently at the man on the ground. He bent over and moved his shirt collar aside, as if inspecting the man's shoulder. He mumbled something.

"What?" She said.

He looked up at her with a quizzical look on his face. "It's a dragon. Breathing fire. Tattooed on his shoulder."

Mhmmm. Is that supposed to mean something? He stood and walked to the front of the wagon, then climbed up. She and the children had to reach out to steady themselves as his weight shifted the wagon. Then, the horses moved and the wheels creaked and groaned. They surged forward.

She noticed, as they moved and picked up speed, that Granthurg kept looking off to the right, back toward where the fight had happened. After a moment, the wagon paused and stopped. It shook again as Granthurg stepped off. "What's happening?" she asked, but didn't get an answer. Then, Granturg appeared in the opening at the back of the wagon with another unconscious man. This one, she recognized as the man in grey that had been following them. She looked up with surprise.

"He's badly hurt, too. I can't just leave him."

Part Six

Distance

64
Oh, No, Not Again...
DeFrantis

It was the sound of lightning and its flash that awoke her. Immediately, low hanging smoke filling the room bit into her eyes and made them water. DeFrantis clenched them closed, then shook her head, and covered her eyes with her hands.

Her hands were heavy, and as she moved them she heard the clinking of metal. She looked down, and in the dim light she saw the shackles on her wrists, each attached to a separate chain. She stretched out her hands, and quickly the chains went taught, attached to something up above her head. She could only move her hands down to about her shoulder level.

She let herself breathe and instantly recognized the smell. *Mage's bane! Again!*

She felt cold, and shivered. The room wasn't drafty, but it was obviously not heated, either. There was another flash in the window, revealing strong rains falling on the glass. *Rain. More rain. The more things change...* She remembered what had happened last time a heavy storm blew across the Wynne River meadows. She had been captured and locked away, just as she was, now. That was how she had met Antonerri.

Antonerri! Her head jumped up, scanning the room. Then she remembered. They had been separated back at the inn, the dark market, when the explosion had gone off. For a moment, her mind lingered on an image of his face.

180

As if on cue, another lightning strike illuminated the room, and she saw another figure asleep against the opposite wall, chained as she was. *Karendle! You're the reason I'm here. You're the reason he's not.*

DeFrantis had crawled across the floor of the dark market place, toward the bleeding and dying Karendle, and tried to save her, tried to use her shadow powers to keep her from slipping into the darkness of death. It had worked, but she looked up and saw the points of swords in her face. Someone was shouting at her, but she couldn't make out any words in the chaos of the moment. Then something had hit the side of her head, hard.

She drooped her hands back against her shoulders, resting them uncomfortably as they dangled by the shackles. *You're the reason I lost sight of the children.*

She took another slow breath, then coughed. The mage's bane smoke made her dizzy. She hung her head. Her mind danced with images of life in the old abandoned chapel with the other street kids. Andrina was the youngest, at about six, and the most playful. But she had gotten a little sick with the rains right before DeFrantis had left to steal some food.

She remembered when Tomanas, who was almost her age, had first told her of the offer to buy the children away. She had been shocked, but he had pressed. "They'll be out of our hair, and we'll have enough to live on for months! Maybe we can even get a real place to stay, and some real food!"

Now here I am, locked away again. I'm of no use to anyone. I'm out of tricks. I'm out of options. Maybe that's just the darkness of the mage's bane telling me what it thinks I want to hear. She yanked on the chains in frustration. They laughed at her with a jangly chuckle.

Or maybe it's the truth.

65
The Prayer of the Wicked
Antonerri

Antonerri picked up a small reed from the cup by the candles. His arm was sore and stiff from the bruising he'd received at the dark market inn. He held the reed in the flame of a candle until it caught a small tongue of its own fire. Then he slowly, painfully, used it to light more candles for his own prayers.

The sanctuary of the cathedral was dark, punctuated only by occasional colorful outbursts of lightning coming in through the stained glass from the storm cascading outside. The room smelled of incense and heating fires. The warm glow of the candles in the rack surrounded him as he knelt down before them.

He bowed his head.

But no words came.

His heart was filled with emptiness. He knelt as an offering, but had nothing to offer his Creator, nothing to give. Only failure.

He heard footsteps behind him, but didn't look up or turn. He heard the rustling of robes as Brother Mathazar also lit a few candles and knelt down beside him.

After a few moments of silence, Brother Mathazar spoke. "We've moved the children you rescued safely to our orphanage. Are you well? You took quite a beating."

Antonerri kept his head bowed in silence.

"But I suspect," Brother Mathazar continued, "That the beating you have taken has been much deeper than what happened yesterday."

Antonerri breathed deeply but still kept his gaze on the candles. "And DeFrantis? Is there any word?"

The brother shook his head, and looked at Antonerri. "They say that confession is good for the soul..."

At that, Antonerri tensed, and stared at the monk. His eyes narrowed, and he hissed with menace, "The last time I was told to confess, to purify my soul, the powers of light were not so cleansing."

Brother Mathazar turned around and sat on the steps of the altar. "I don't know what you've been through, or what you may have done. I don't claim to have any answers, either. I'm just offering a chance for you to unburden."

Antonerri looked him over, then returned his eyes to the candles. "I am unworthy. But I don't understand it. I have been cast from the church, and my own powers have left me," He took a breath, "And I have no idea why. My greatest sin is to defend the weak, to fight for those that can't fight for themselves. Isn't that what we're supposed to do?"

The brother nodded.

Antonerri continued, "So what great sin am I guilty of? Why has the Creator abandoned me?" The rain blew on the windows as he fell silent again.

"Has He?"

Antonerri glared at him again, with a quizzical brow.

"I don't know, but it seems to me that he's still using you to help the weak. You have saved three children from the depths of misery. You have three friends who value you enough to save you, and it looks like there is at least one other friend that needs your strength now. I wonder how they all feel about your 'worthiness'." He reached out, grasped Antonerri's shoulder, and patted it in reassurance. Then he pressed on it to support himself as he stood. "I'll bet they lean on you, too."

He stepped away from the altar. "I'll leave you to your prayers."

184

66

The Dragon's Flame
Granthurg

The rain wasn't hard, but it was steady, forming pools and streams in the street. Grathurg and Thissraelle held their cloaks tightly as they moved through the dark from the cathedral to the wharf.

"Slow down a little!" Thissraelle complained, "Where are you going?"

"Back to the barge. And I don't want to be seen." He said, glancing back over his shoulder. She ran a few steps to catch up to him.

"What's at the barge?"

"Answers, I hope." He kept up his stride. *Assuming everything is still there.*

They approached the wharf. The waterfront in Dirae was a few street blocks long, and there were several docking ports for boats and barges. There were crates and boxes all along the street above the docks, and Granthurg slipped between them to cover his movement. It wasn't easy, as tall as he was. Thissraelle followed suit.

"You OK?" He asked, as they paused behind some cargo at the top of the dock. She nodded. He looked up and down the riverfront, illuminated by a couple of bright oculi suspended on poles high above the wharf structure. He moved quickly, but carefully down the slippery dock to his barge. When he got there he stepped onto it, and helped Thissraelle. He immediately moved past their own cargo toward the steering platform at the stern. As he did, he saw that the boxes and crates had been untethered and tossed around. Many had been opened, with their contents strewn over the deck, now soaked and ruined. He heard Thissraelle say, "What happened here?"

Granthurg stepped over the clutter and said, "They've been here. I knew it. They probably searched here when their man didn't come back from the dark market. I'm glad we were safe up in the Cathedral."

He stepped up onto the platform, under the tarp. The noise of the rain beating on it was oppressive. One of the barge's lighting oculi had been taken, and the other was dim, making it hard to see. Before him on the deck was his trunk, opened and overturned. He sighed and bent down, righting it. He knelt and began putting scrolls and clothing back into the trunk. Thissraelle knelt next to him and helped. He said, "Some of these got a little wet from the rain. Still, it looks like they're not badly damaged." They latched the trunk closed.

"Is that what you wanted? Your scrolls?" Thissraelle asked.

"Yes, partly." *But there's more.* Before she could ask, Granthurg had turned around and stepped off the stern of the barge, landing in the river with a huge splash.

"Granthurg!" Thissraelle scrambled to the edge of the platform, and looked over just as his head bobbed up out of the water. He spat and shook the drops from his face, a gesture that was a bit useless in the rain. Then he rose up and stood on the bottom. The water was just below his shoulder. He smiled up at her. "It's not that deep here." He stepped forward, then ducked his head as he passed under the barge, between the long floats that kept it buoyant. He felt along the floats as he moved further into the darkness, his hands searching.

"Are you OK back there?" Thissraelle was leaning over, with the rain falling on her head, trying to look over the edge.

His hands found a box, and he reached up to untie it. Once it was freed, he held it over his head and moved through the water back to the stern. His boots were slow on the slippery, muddy riverbed as he ducked to come out from under the barge.

He handed it up to Thissraelle. It was a small, wooden box, only a few feet long and a half a foot wide. She set it on the platform.

"Can you lift me up?" Granthurg said with a smile. Thissraelle laughed a little at the irony, then extended her hand. Nothing happened. Granthurg looked up, blinking in the rain.

"Hang on", she said, and refocused. Her hand began glowing slightly with a shade of blue, and Granthurg raised up, dripping, until he was even with the platform. He hovered there, and shook most of the water out of his shirt and pants, then stepped onto the barge. He knelt and reached for the box, being careful not to drip on it.

"What is it?" Thisraelle leaned in to look.

"I don't know. It's Rinkmoor's. I suspect it's what these attackers have been after, so I hid it that night that everyone else slept in the inn." Granthurg set it in front of him. "It's not mine, so I didn't want to open it. But if our life is at risk, I need to know what we're dealing with." He looked at her, as if for approval, or reassurance. She nodded.

He reached to his right and grabbed a small metal wrench from the deck, and easily twisted off the lock. Gently, he raised the lid.

Inside was a beautifully ornate dagger, with a curved white blade and a finely stitched leather hilt, set on soft black velvet. Granthurg picked it up and turned it in his hands. The blade looked like ivory, but not like any he had seen before, and was etched with intricate and overlapping lines. The crosspiece was a dark metal and shaped like two arms with clawed hands. The pommel at the end was a large disc with a pattern carved into it. Granthurg turned it in the dim light to see it better, and sharply drew in his breath. "Oh, Rinkmorr, what have you gotten yourself into?"

"What?" Thisraelle asked, "What is it?"

He turned the blade to show her the design. It was a dragon, breathing fire.

67
It's a Long Story
Karendle

A stroke of lightning hit very close, with a bright flash and loud clap. Karendle jolted awake with a shout, a gasp, and a jangle of chains. The room was dark once again, and she tried in vain to see her surroundings. She could hear rain pelting windows, but could see no light from them. The air was thick with a heavy, musky incense that was difficult to breathe. The floor below her legs was cold, hard stone. She tried to stand, but the chains on her wrists, over her head, prevented her. She moved her legs under her and sat up against the wall that held her shackles.

"So, you're awake now." A voice spoke to her from across a

room. She tried to focus her eyes in the direction. It was female, and it sounded familiar. It carried a tone of anger, though, that she didn't quite recognize.

"Who are you?" The smoke made Karendle cough when she first spoke. "Where are you?"

"I'm right here. I'm chained to the wall, like you are." DeFrantis replied. "And you know who I am."

Karendle was surprised. "I do?"

"You've been chasing me for over a week, now, but I have no idea why. I would say that you had finally caught me, but it looks like you're just as caught as I am!"

Silence fell again, with a weight that hung like the smoke in the thick air. The only sound was the rain. Lightning struck again, more distant, but still bright enough to flash through the windows and illuminate the room. She recognized DeFrantis in the shadows from across the floor, and she looked away.

Her mind was clearing, now, as she became more fully awake. She remembered things, images. *You were running from the guard tower, and I threw a blast at you. You were on the barge when I captured the other wizard in the stone, and when we traveled up the river. You, the giant, the elf girl, and the other man. You were there at the dark market when I got my oculi back from the thief. You were there when he stabbed me...*

"You were the one that healed me!"

"Yes. Yes, I was."

After a pause in the darkness, Karendle asked, "Why did you save me?"

"I don't know. I really don't know. Maybe you can tell me why you were trying to kill me!"

"I wasn't trying to kill you!"

"A couple of fireballs say otherwise!"

"That wasn't meant for you!" Karendle thought that over, "At least, the one in the market wasn't..." The rain again filled the empty spaces in between their words. "Maybe I'd better explain."

"Yes. Maybe that would be a good idea. Take your time. I'm not going anywhere." Karendle heard DeFrantis' chains rattle, as if she were settling in for a long story.

68
It's a Long, Long Story
Karendle

Karendle pushed herself back up against the wall, and brought her knees up to her chest. The chains on her wrists made that difficult. The stone masonry was cold against her back.

How can I tell her? I was trying to capture her, not kill her! But, I would have sold her out just like the slavers. And my contacts told me not to tell anyone. But she saved my life. I owe her at least that much, don't I? But where do I start? She thought for a moment, then began.

"I came to Twynne Rivers from the western mountains because I wanted to learn to do magic. Ever since I was little I wanted it. I

190

went to the wizard's guild, but they wouldn't take me. I'm part Dwarf, and Dwarves don't 'do' magic. Or at least the High Elves in the guild don't think so. Then, I met a couple of humans who told me how I could do magic right away, and even get back at the guild. I was thrilled! They showed me these stones, gems, that gave me magic."

"Oculi?"

"Yep. They showed me how to use them, a little. Then, they told me that I had to go capture wizards. Two of the stones they gave me, gray, dark stones, were just for that."

"That's how you zapped the one on the barge?"

"Yes. They said that wizards are evil and are ruining our city. They said they'd pay me well for every wizard I brought them. So, I set out on my task. I heard about a shadow wizard that had been caught stealing from a local inn, and I figured that would be an easy start."

"So, that was me."

Karendle hesitated. "That was you. I lost you for a while after you ran from the tower. I wasn't trying to kill you. I was trying to catch you. I didn't really know how to use the stones. I guess I still don't. I lost you, anyway, but found you back at the waterfront on Grunthos' barge."

"Granthurg." DeFrantis corrected.

"Yeah. Him." Karendle took a breath, choked, and coughed. She shifted against the wall. "So, when the fight started, I thought it was others coming after you. I rushed in. When the other wizards

191

showed up, and I still don't know why, I suddenly had a chance to get a guild wizard! And it worked! I was so excited! The guys that hired me were pretty pleased as well. I was going to take him back to Twynne Rivers and get paid. I would have been out of your life completely. But then...."

DeFrantis didn't like the pause. "But then... what?"

"They told me to go back. They wanted Thissarill, or whatever her name is. I guess she's a big deal for the wizard's guild or something. They told me to capture her. I don't really know why." *I don't really know why I'm doing any of this.* "But before I could get back to the inn, I was robbed, and he stole my pouch with all of my gems. I had to get it back, so I tracked him to the dark market, where the slavers were. You have to understand, my whole new life was given to me in that pouch, and taken from me when he robbed me! I fought him and I grabbed it. That second blast was meant for him, not you. I grabbed my oculi and blasted him, just out of sheer spite. It didn't work. I missed him. He rushed me and stabbed me instead. He would have killed me."

Karendle fell silent for a moment.

DeFrantis spoke in an even, but short tone. "In the chaos you created, I lost sight of the children being sold. I had hoped that they would lead me to the children I've been looking for. Now I have no idea what happened to any of them. I have no idea what happened to Antonerri, either."

Karendle dropped her head to her hands. The smoke irritated her eyes. "I'm so sorry. I was only worried about myself. Now here's the mess I've gotten us into."

The awkward stillness was as thick as the smoke. Only the steady rain and the occasional lightning flash cut through the haze.

69
It's Not Just a Dagger
Granthurg

It was mid-morning, but it was still dark and gloomy outside of the cathedral hall. Where normally the rising sun would have streamed bright colors through the eastern stained glass windows, like it had just the day before, now thick rainclouds made it almost as dark as the night. Rain streamed down from those windows, beating with the winds against the panes.

Granthurg sat at a table that had been set up in the back of the sanctuary, strewn with scrolls and a few books. The corner was lit by a few oculus lanterns, creating a glow that made the pages shine and fed his hunger for understanding.

The Dragon's Flame. The Dragon's Flame... He leaned back in the chair and heard it creak with strain under his huge weight. He wiped his face with his hands and rubbed his eyes.

He reached over and picked up the ivory dagger. He hefted it, musing. *Why does everyone seem to want you bad enough to kill for you?*

When he and Thissraelle had gotten back from the barge late last night, he had wanted to break open his scrolls immediately. Thissraelle had convinced him to get some sleep first. He agreed, but didn't sleep that much, and got up early anyway. The few resident monks were already moving about and attending to their daily lives, and helped him to set up the table. As he began to spread out his scrolls, they had mentioned that the Father kept a small library in his chambers there at the cathedral.

Granthurg set the blade back down and turned a few more pages in the tome he had been looking through. It seemed to be records and observations kept by the Father about religious influences in the south of Wynne.

He turned another page and looked at its title: *How Can We Justify the Sacerdotis Confesoris? What?* He read about the tortures used to extract confessions by some in the city of Twynne Rivers. Intrigued, he turned the page again, but there was no more on the topic. *I wonder if this is why Antonerri and DeFrantis didn't want to come here to the cathedral.*

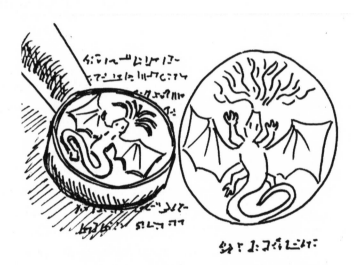

He turned a page, then another, skipping ahead to see if there were more on the topic, then stopped, staring at a drawing on the page. *That's it! That's the dragon breathing flame!* It was a drawing of a dragon with spread wings holding its head up, blowing tongues of fire up into the sky, the whole image surrounded by a circle. He picked up the blade and turned it to place the pommel next to the drawing. The dragon's tails were curled in different loops, and the flames flickered with differing tongues, but they were too similar to be a coincidence.

The door to the sanctuary creaked as it swung open. Brother Mathazar stepped in. "I'm sorry to bother you. It's so good to have company here, so we love to accommodate whenever we do!"

Granturg looked up, distracted. A man stepped in behind the Brother, the man Granthurg had fought in the field the day before. He walked with a bit of a limp and soreness, and his hands and feet were chained. His face was down, and he didn't look nearly as threatening as he had then. The fact that he was flanked by two armed and armored town guards ready to take him into custody made him even less so.

Brother Mathazar shrugged. "He said he wanted to talk to you before he left." He stepped back, and nodded to the two guards before gently closing the door. It clicked in the heavy, awkward silence.

Finally, without looking up, the man spoke. "You brought me back here and had me healed." Granthurg just looked at him closely, until he continued. "I couldn't move. You could have easily left me there in the meadow, in pain, for the wolves. Now, I'm alive. I can walk." He looked at the shackles on his wrist.

He looked up at Granthurg and the things on the table, seeing the dagger. He smiled a little. "I guess you do have it, after all."

Granthurg laughed and picked it up. "This isn't mine. My boss-- My friend owns it. I had no idea this was what all of you were after. I don't know what it is, still."

The man shrugged. "Others will still come after it. Lots of people want it. Lots of powerful people. Lots of people who aren't powerful enough, yet." He looked at Granthurg and smiled. "But don't worry. I won't tell them you have it. I'll tell them it's gone. I owe you that much." The guards looked at each other with uneasy glances, then pulled on the chains, moving him toward the door. "Looks like I've got to go."

"Yes," Granthurg replied, adding, "Bless your steps." The man nodded, accepting the blessing, and moved away, chains clinking on the floorboards. The guards opened the sanctuary door with a creak.

"A question for you!" Granthurg blurted. The man stopped and looked back. "You said I was going to sell this to The Dragon's Flame. Who is that?"

He nodded. "I only know what I've heard. I was sent from Twynne Rivers and I don't know Dirae very well. But it's said that they're a dark and dangerous cult that worships dragons. I think they were tangled up with the slavers at the old inn. Don't let them know that you have that blade. I'll bet that won't go well for you." He took in a breath, then bowed his head slightly toward Granthurg. "Bless your steps."

Granturg nodded, and the man stepped through door. As it closed, Granthurg looked back down to the image on the page.

Worships dragons?

196

70

Magic, or No Magic
DeFrantis

The morning had dawned, but the rain fell on. It was still dark, but some light was getting through the clouds, the trees, and, ultimately, the windows. DeFrantis could finally see across the dim and hazy room. It was not as large as an open hall in a castle, but it had a high ceiling and walls, each decorated with several tall windows. Tapestries and curtains hung around in the shadows of the room. It looked like the place had once been a manor for a well-to-do noble, but it hadn't been cared for in years. There were no furniture pieces, only a few pillars reaching upward into the darkness from the stone floor.

Karendle was slouched against the far wall, with her wrists and forearms dangling by the chains in front of her. Her head was tipped, and her breathing was heavy.

Well, I'm glad one of us can sleep, at least. I guess it's about time we figure out what we're going to do.

"Hey!" She called out, trying to rouse Karendle. There was no response. "Hey! Wake up!" Her head bobbed a little.

"Karendle! Hey!"

"What? Wha -?" Karende raised up and blinked.

"Wake up!"

Karendle lifted her hands and ran them over her face and through her hair, shaking the chains as she did. DeFrantis could barely see the outline of her face and her short, stocky form in the shadows. She heard a grunt.

DeFrantis spoke first, "I'm hungry and I want to find my kids. I don't know why they didn't just kill us outright, but we're here, we're alive, and I'm wanting to get out of here."

There was silence for a moment, as Karendle shook herself awake. " OK, great. I'm all for that. How do we do it? Can you wizard up a way out of these shackles?"

"Not with all this mage's bane in the air."

"Huh? Mage's bane? What's that?"

"It's what's making all the smoke that's been choking up your lungs. It blocks your ability to use magic."

The wind had picked up a little and was blowing the rain more fiercely against the windows. There were no thunderclaps, though, with this storm. Karendle mumbled, "Do you think they'll bring us anything to eat? If someone does, maybe one of us could overcome him and get a key." She yanked on her chains either to test them or simply to punctuate her thought. "That would be pretty difficult, though."

Karendle continued, "Maybe Antonerri or that Giant guy have been looking for us. Maybe we'll get rescued."

DeFrantis wasn't very hopeful. "I don't even know where we are. How would they find us?" *How would they find us. Are they even looking? Did Antonerri even survive the fight?* She shook her head, her heart sinking at that thought.

Karendle interrupted her dark reverie. "Too bad we can't send them a message, right?"

Send them a message! DeFrantis' head shot up, her eyes suddenly alert. "Hey, when you were back in town, how did you contact the men who had hired you?" Her voice was quick, suddenly intense.

"What?"

"You said you told them you'd caught a wizard, right? And they told you to go back for Thissraelle, right?"

"Yesss...."

"So how did you contact them?"

"I used an oculus. A blue gem. I just focused on it, and I spoke with them."

"Great!"

"But isn't that magic? I thought you said we can't do magic with all this something bane smokey stuff!"

DeFrantis' mind was rushing through a thousand thoughts at once. "But the priest used powers! He blasted Antonerri over and over! How did he do it?" Her mind began running through her memories of that night.

"What priest?" Karendle sat up, confused. "What are you talking about?"

DeFrantis pictured the Confessor Priest, standing outside her cell, in an elaborate white robe. She saw him turn and shout at

Antonerri, and raised his staff. *His staff had a glowing gemstone!* "An oculus! There was an oculus on the staff! Maybe the mage's bane doesn't stop powers from oculi!"

Karendle's confused look made DeFrantis say it again. "I think we can use your oculi! If that's true, we might be able to contact them! Thissraelle uses the powers of the mind, maybe we can reach her with your blue gem!"

"Well, that may well be, but I don't have it. They took my pouch when they captured us." Karendle slumped again. She had gotten a bit caught up in the excitement.

"Well, maybe they didn't."

"Come again?"

DeFrantis shifted her weight, raising herself up on her legs. She reached through her collar, deep under her shirt. It was tricky to reach, because the chains restricted her movement, but in a moment she pulled out her hand and a leather pouch with a drawstrap. She held it out toward Karendle.

"Is this what you're talking about?"

71
A Gem of an Idea
Karendle

"That's it!" Karendle gasped. "That's my pouch! How did you get it?"

DeFrantis smiled. "I picked it up off the floor after I healed you. I didn't know what it was, but you were reaching for it when I got

200

to you. I figured it was important. I didn't even have a chance to look in it."

"They didn't take it from you when they hauled us away?"

"When you're a street kid, you learn where to hide stuff that's been stolen." DeFrantis chuckled. "I've got your dagger, too."

Karendle looked surprised. "I didn't have a dagger..."

"Yes, you did. Stuck between your ribs. It's a pretty small one." She shifted on the floor. "I'm not sure I could reach it right now, though."

She held the pouch in her hands in front of her and began to untie the leather strap. It wasn't easy with her hands suspended by the chains. She looked in the pouch. "I can't see very well. There looks like one, two, three stones."

They looked at each other for a moment, and Karendle nodded. "I'd like to fix this. Can you throw me the pouch?"

DeFrantis nodded and re-tied the strap. She wound it up into as small and tight of a bundle as she could, then tossed it. The chains rattled and snapped her arm back. The pouch flew about halfway across the room, then slid a few more feet, still a good distance from Karendle.

Karendle swore an old dwarvish curse. She reached out with her leg to try and scoot it towards her, but couldn't reach it.

"Try again," DeFrantis called out. Karendle scooted herself as far from the wall as she could and tried to lay flat on the ground. She stretched her legs out and pointed her toes at the pouch. It was close, but still not enough.

Grunting with pain, she pulled against the chains and reached again, this time able to nudge the pouch with her toes. She carefully pressed on it and shifted it slightly toward her before her foot slipped off. Her arms were hurting in their sockets, as they had to both reach and support her weight. She reached again and was able to move it closer a few more inches.

She slouched, gasping for breath.

"One more try!"

As she drew in breaths, the smoke from the incense made her cough. She took in a breath, and held it as she reached her toes past the pouch and drew it toward her. Then, panting, and coughing, she shifted back to the wall, moving the pouch with her foot along the way. Finally, she sat again, with the pouch in front of her.

"Great. Now how am I going to pick it up?" She looked at DeFrantis, who just shrugged. *There's gotta be a way to do this.* She looked down at the pouch on the floor between her outstretched legs, right between her knees. *My knees...*

She used her feet to push herself and the pouch as close to the wall as she could, then, using the chains as a support, pulled her legs behind her and got up until she was kneeling. *Yes! Yes, this can work!*

"What are you doing? Are you getting it?"

Karendle didn't answer. She moved her knees together, pressing the pouch between them. She pressed hard, gripping it as tight as

202

she could. Then, with a grunt, she pulled on the chains, lifting herself up off the floor slightly. She flipped her legs out from under her and dropped herself back to the floor. She closed her knees to her chest, and fell back against the wall, again panting and coughing from the exertion and the smoke.

"What did you do?"

Karendle opened her eyes and saw the pouch sitting snug between her upraised knees. She reached down with one hand, straining against the chains and took the pouch in her fingers. She gingerly lifted it up and took it securely in both hands and finally relaxed her back and legs. As she slouched, she untied the strap and shook the stones out onto her hand. Two gray stones and a blue gem.

"I got them!" She held them up for Karendle to see. "I got them!"

She looked at them and held them as if she was holding her whole life. *The red one's gone. I must've dropped it when he attacked. Oh, well. The blue one's right here. And here's the stone with the wizard.* She looked at it intently, as if she were trying to see him inside of it.

She shook off her thoughts and put the two gray stones back in the pouch, holding tight to the sapphire. She set the pouch on her shoulder and held the blue stone up before her. She looked across the dim fog at DeFrantis. Her friend smiled and nodded slowly.

OK. Here we go.

She turned her focus to the gem, and to Thissraelle.

"What are you waiting for, child?" Brother Mathazar's question interrupted her thoughts. "Eat! Eat!"

She startled, then looked back down at her bowl of stew. The smell of the rich brown broth wafted up into her face, and the meat and vegetables looked appetizing as well. Beside her steaming bowl was a torn half-loaf of bread. She picked up her spoon and smiled. "Thank you!"

"What has your mind so enraptured?"

She looked over at him, then at the others. Next to him were two other monks each dipping into their own bowls, and across from them sat Antonerri and Granthurg. The giant was, at least, eagerly slurping on his stew, alternating mouthfuls with the bread. The sight of him stuffing his mouth made Thissraelle giggle.

He stopped for only a moment. "What?"

She smiled and took a spoonful of stew. It was delicious and full of savory flavors. She swallowed and reached for her bread.

"I've just been thinking of all that's happened to us. How we all came to be in this place, and now all that we are finding out about the Dragon's Flame." She raised the bread. "It's kind of overwhelming." She took a bite.

"True. You'll no doubt be wanting to find your other friends as well."

Antonerri raised his gaze as he heard that, and Thissraelle nodded. She lifted her spoon again.

"Are you there?"

Thissraelle's head jumped up and looked around, confused.

"Are you there? Can you hear me?"

She dropped her spoon with a clatter and stood up from the table. She looked frantically around the room.

Granthurg said, "Thissraelle! What's wrong?"

"I know that voice!" She whispered. "Where is she?"

"You CAN hear me! Talk to me!"

Thisraelle shook her head and closed her eyes. *She's in my head.*

"Yes! I am!"

Where are you? Are you well?

"DeFrantis is with me! We're captured! We need your he--"

"Where are you?" The others at the table stared at her outburst. Her mind fell silent. Frantically, she cleared her thoughts and opened herself up. She looked around the table, trying to find support. "Where ARE YOU?" She shouted again.

"I'm sorry. I'm so sorr--"

No! Come back! Talk to me! Where are you? Her mind, her thoughts were silent. The connection was gone.

She stepped away from the table and closed her eyes. She raised her hands out to her side and began slowly turning.

Granthurg stood. "Thissraelle, are you OK?"

"They reached out to me. They contacted me."

"Who?" All eyes were on her as she slowly turned. Her hands and head began to slowly glow with an azure halo.

"Karendle." She kept turning, then stopped. "And DeFrantis."

Antonerri jumped to his feet. "DeFrantis! Where?"

Thissraelle moved one arm before her to point. "That way. I don't know how far, but they're that way." They all looked where she pointed, out the rain-spattered window into the cloudy dark beyond.

73
There They Are!
Granthurg

Antonerri pushed the plates, dishes, and food aside to clear a space on the table. He wasn't too gentle about it, as plates clanked and bits of flatware clattered onto the floor. With a thump and a slight grunt, Granthurg dropped an armload of books and half-loose scrolls onto the table. He began rustling through them as everyone gathered behind him.

After a moment, Granthurg found the particular scroll he was looking for and laid it onto the table, rolling one end out. He

206

paused, then rolled the other end up, and scooted the scroll back to do it again.

"There we go!" He stood up, looking down at the drawing on the table. It was a map, and fairly detailed. "So, this is Wynne. It's a really old map, but it'll help. This is Twynne Rivers, and here are the two branches of the Greater and Lesser Wynne Rivers. All over this area, you can see that land dotted with manors and villages. Over here is the southern part of the Umbrawood forest. If you follow the northern Wynne River along here, you'll get to Dirae. That's where we are right now."

He spun around, trying to orient himself, and mumbled, "Which way is East?"

Antonerri jumped up, too, and pointed, "Well, that door leads into the main sanctuary, so, the front door would be--" He turned a little, "--there. Then--" He turned a little back the other way, "That would be East."

Granthurg nodded agreement, and leaned back over the maps. He took the two scroll sticks, lifted the map, and oriented it on the tabletop to line the map's Eastern direction to the way Antonerri had been pointing.

Antonerri joined him at the table. "Thissraelle! Which way to DeFrantis again?"

Everyone looked at Thisraelle as she pointed south-east out the window of the hall, toward the river, and the forest. Then he she closed her eyes and took deep breaths. After a moment, she adjusted her arm slightly. "That way."

"Hold that!" Granthurg said, and began tracing a line from Dirae that followed the general direction of Thissraelle's arm.

"Just a minute." Antonerri drew his sword and laid the straight edge of the blade at Dirae. He turned it, glancing up to match the direction as close a he could to Thissraelle's arm. "Like this?"

Thissraelle looked down and nodded.

They all looked as Granthurg's finger followed the edge of the blade across the river and into the forest. Soon it touched a spot marked with a shield and some small writing. Granthurg squinted close and read, "Barony of Westwood."

"What's that?" Thissraelle asked. Everyone looked at each other, but nobody, including the friars, had ever heard of it.

"Hold on..." Granthurg moved a few of the scrolls and grabbed a tome he'd been reading. It was labelled "Wynne". "This is where I found out about the dagger!" He began flipping the pages.

Antonerri glanced over at Thissraelle with a hopeful look. "Is this where DeFrantis is?" Thissraelle just shrugged, but smiled, anyway.

"THERE! Oh, by the Creator!" Granthurg called out, and pointed at the page. It was full of shields, coats of arms, and at the top was the title "Heraldry of House Twynnham of Wynne". Granthurg was pointing to a crest. The others looked at the page, at his insistent finger, then up at Granthurg. They didn't share his moment of clarity. "That crest was carved into the side of the wagon we took from the slave market! I didn't think much of it at the time, because the wood planks were weathered and it was hard to recognize the charge. I assumed it was a gryphon or a lion or something. But I've figured it out! I know where they are!"

Antonerri glanced back down at the page, at the crest under Granthurg's large tapping finger. "It's a dragon!"

74
Over the River and Through The Wood
Antonerri

Thankfully, the rain had stopped by the time they were ready to travel. It was still overcast, and dark, and the rain had made the ruts of the wagon's path very muddy. Still the horses were strong and pulled them forward.

"This must be a path they've traveled many times. They seem familiar with it." Antonerri commented. Granthurg nodded.

Getting across the Wynne had been a fairly simple task as well, using Granthurg's barge. Clearing off the ransacked rubble to make room for the wagon was not as easy and had taken much of the rest of the morning. Then they began the journey into the southern deep of the Umbrawood Forest.

It was dark inside the forest, partly because of the overcast skies, and partly because of the thick canopy of trees which gave the forest its name. The leaves had just come on to the trees about a month before, and were thick and strong. It was clear that this path was used, but not used very much. There was some underbrush, much of it new growth, but it wasn't high enough to impede movement. Even so, the ground below was uneven, and full of old tree roots and it made travel bumpy and a bit noisy. A thick layer of last winter's dead leaves, now wet from the spring rains, was helping the wagon get through the mud. It gave a musty smell to the trail.

"I don't understand." Antonerri asked, "What is the significance of the Dragons? Who is this 'Dragon's Flame' we're hearing about?"

Granthurg was thoughtful before responding, "Yeah, I don't know, either. I'm trying to put it all together in my mind. There are some histories I remember. Some I read, and some I was told as a kid. They say that the Dragons used to rule this land."

Antonerri was surprised at this. Thissraelle stirred in the back of the wagon and leaned forward between them to hear the story.

"Even before the Mage Kings of the High Elves. The story goes that they were quite oppressive and enslaved the humans for generations. Then they started dying off, and nobody knew why. The humans and the elves finally overthrew them, and that's when the elven Mage Kings began ruling Wynne. Now, of course, it's all fractured. It's like each group has divided up into its own space."

He paused and thought. "I'm not sure what the 'Dragon's Flame' is. The man who attacked me said they were cultists that worship dragons. There are still dragons in Wynne, but not many live, and few people ever see them."

Thissraelle took this in. Antonerri looked at his companions then down at the horses and the trail before them.

"I'm so grateful to know you two. Your knowledge, and," He gestured to Thisraelle, "Your magic has been a great help. I hope we can get to DeFrantis before..." His voice trailed off.

Granthurg smiled and put a huge hand on Antonerri's shoulder. "Don't worry, friend. We're here with you."

210

Thissraelle added, "We take care of each other. We'll find them. Once we're closer, I'll be able to place them and hopefully I can open a dimensional portal straight to them." She paused, and sighed. "That may, however, take most of my will. I'm not sure how useful I'll be in a fight after that."

Granthurg gave Antonerri's shoulder a friendly shove. "Getting us there will be a great help. Leave the fighting to us. That will be our job!"

"Once we find DeFrantis, hopefully then we'll be able to find the children she's looking for." He smiled at his new friends. *Isn't this what I always wanted? Why I joined the Holy Guard? To fight for those that could not fight for themselves?*

But there was a fear inside him as well. A fear of the unknown. *What are we getting into? What's waiting for us? Am I up to this? We'll need the blessings of the Creator for this, and I'm not yet sure I deserve that.*

The wagon rumbled and creaked along the dark, hidden path.

Part Seven

Reunion

75
Oh, To Breathe Again
DeFrantis

"I wish I wasn't so hungry," DeFrantis heard Karendle say, across the darkness, "Because this gruel tastes absolutely horrible."

I've had worse. DeFrantis thought about that for a moment. *Actually, I'm not so sure of that.* She carefully held the bowl close to her face, partly because the chains holding her wrist high wouldn't let her hold it any other way, and partly because that was the only way to use fingers from her other chained hand to scoop the meal into her mouth.

"Is it really this bad," Karendle continued, "Or is it the mage's bane smoke that makes it taste like this?"

DeFrantis carefully wiped the last of the gruel from the wooden bowl with her fingers and then licked them clean. *Disgusting. But having something in my stomach is a good thing. Something. Anything.*

I wish I'd had a bit of time to prepare. If I'd known when they were going to feed us, I might have been able to figure out a way to snatch a key from the guard. The last time that had happened, with the Confessor Priest and his guard, it was kind of improvised. Maybe it was her hunger and her bane-addled mind, but she hadn't seen an opportunity to move on this time.

"You're very quiet."

DeFrantis raised her gaze. Even though the rain had stopped, the sun had also set, shrouding the entire room in darkness. She squinted to try and see where Karendle had been, where the voice was coming from. There was only shadow and smoke. She dropped the bowl to her lap, and it rolled off and clattered onto the floor.

"So, you're awake? You're done eating? Are you lost in thought?"

DeFrantis shifted her aching back, breathed deep, and then coughed. "Yeah. Just thinking."

"...About...?"

"I'm just trying to think of a way to get us out of these chains."

"That would be nice." Karendle agreed. "I hope they can find us soon."

214

"Yes, well, that really would be nice. But, honestly," DeFrantis tensed her chains, "I'm getting a bit tired of waiting. If I could just use my shadow power, I could make short work of these locks. If I could just clear my head!"

"This smoke is just so thick. It's hard to breathe, much less to think!"

"Well, that's how the incense works. It makes your head all foggy, and suppresses your will. It makes you despair, if you let it." DeFrantis crossed her arms and held her shoulders, as if to comfort herself.

"Yeah. I get it. What I wouldn't give for one breath of fresh air."

Yeah. Fresh air. To breathe deep and feel alive.

Fresh air.

Fresh Air!

"Fresh air!"

"What?"

"If we can somehow break a window or open a door, that might bring in enough air to restore even a part of our will!" *That's what happened the minute we opened the door to the holding rooms in the guard tower back in Twynne Rivers! The moment I got good breath in my lungs, I felt my will return!* "Help me, Karendle! Help me think of something! Is there something we can throw at a window? Maybe someway to wedge the door open when they come in. Anything?"

There was silence as they both tried to think. DeFrantis began to twist and squirm against the chains, trying to see if she could reach where she had hidden the dagger.

Karendle said, "What about the oculi? Can you use any of them? Can you use their will?"

"Are any of them onyx? For shadow?"

"No, and I only know how to use the sapphire for connection. I don't know if it can be used to move things."

"Too bad you lost the red one. You could just blow up the chains."

"Yes, but..." Karendle's voice trailed off in the dark.

DeFrantis stopped struggling. "...But what?"

"What if someone else broke the window, or opened the door?"

DeFrantis squinted. "What are you talking about."

"I just remembered that I have someone trapped in this stone..."

76
Am I Evil?
Karendle

"What? Who?" DeFrantis asked, then gasped with realization, "The wizard you caught on the barge!"

Karendle just nodded, not really thinking that DeFrantis probably couldn't see her. She was lost in her thoughts as she held the

216

polished stone in her hands. Her dwarven eyes could see a bit in the dark, and she looked at it.

This was to be my new life. A wizard hunter. I was going to get back at the Wizard's Guild. The others were going to pay me well for him. I was going to be able to prove myself. This stone holds all of my opportunity, my future. Should I set all of that free? Should I let it go?

"Can you loose him? Give it a try!"

It also holds a person. A person I trapped. A person I don't even know. He's a wizard, and one of the Guild, even! Wizards are evil, right? Like DeFrantis. She's a wizard, of sorts. But she used magic and saved me. And she's just trying to save the kids. She's been trying to save them their whole life. How can that be evil?

She felt the smooth, polished surface under her fingers. It was round and gray, like a stone out of a river. *I caught him. I reached out with this stone, and caught him, just like an animal in a trap. I was going to sell him. I would have taken him and sold him to my own connection, in my own little dark market, just like the slavers and thieves were doing. Selling people. Real people. And children!*

Does that make me evil? As that thought hit her, she recoiled. *I'm not evil! Am I?*

"Karendle? Are you alright?"

Karendle took a breath before she said, "Why did I let myself get trapped in their game?" DeFrantis didn't respond, and Karendle didn't honestly expect a response.

No more! I choose the game, now. I choose the moves!

She clenched her eyes and gripped the oculus tight in her determined fist. She stretched out the hand holding the oculus and focused on it. Even using the will embedded in the oculus was difficult with the mage's bane, but after a moment she felt a shiver, and the stone began to glow with a silvery light. The light grew, and Karendle opened her eyes. She could see across the room, into DeFrantis' delighted face.

The silvery glow leapt from the stone, in the direction of Karendle's point, and settled on the floor, surrounding a reclining body. He was wearing the same dark pants and loose blue shirt he had on the day of the fight on the barge. He lay still until the glow subsided, when he began groaning and rolled over. He breathed, then coughed, hard. He gasped for breath, rasping and finally crawling up on his hands and knees.

"By the Creator!" he wheezed. He tried to look around, sat back on his heels, and finally said, "Where am I?"

DeFrantis just giggled. "We're not entirely sure, either!"

77
Am I Dead?
Eddiwarth

Eddiwarth raked his hair out of his eyes and tried to blink away the burning. Something was irritating them. He coughed again, then twice more. *Smoke. That's what's making my eyes hurt.* He coughed again, though not as hard, and was finally able to see, albeit with a bit of a blur. His head hurt.

He turned his head toward the voice he had just heard. He squinted, and saw the shadowy form of a person sitting by a pillar. "Who are you?"

"I'm DeFrantis." It was a feminine voice, fairly young. He blinked and wiped his eyes clear. His elvish vision helped him see a bit better in the dark, too. It was a young lady, wearing dark clothes, and her hands were chained to the pillar. "We need your help."

"Who is 'we'?" His voice was still rough from the thick incense in the room. The smell had a sickly sweet note, and it made it hard for him to breathe, and hard to think.

"That would be me. My name is Karendle." The voice from behind his back startled him, and he quickly spun around. Defensively, he raised his hand, and raised thoughts of fire in his mind. He tried to channel those through his fingers, but there was nothing there. The thoughts and will were weak and empty. No flames, no magic. Nothing.

He looked at his hand and his fingers. *Why didn't that work? Maybe I'm dead. I've been killed, and I'm dead.*

"Did you just try to blast me?" Karendle's voice continued, "Well, I can't say that I'd blame you. But it won't work here."

"What?"

The other voice, DeFrantis, said, "Yeah, that smoke you're breathing is choking off more than your voice. Your magic's gone, too."

These voices sound familiar. I've heard them, but I don't remember where. Where have I been? He coughed a few more times, then rasped to clear his throat. He crawled aside, so that he wasn't trapped in between the two women.

Memories started coming back to him. *I was with Hamrisonn in the city. We were looking for someone. I don't remember who.*

I was on a river barge. He and I were after something, or someone. It was there. I floated down to get it, and suddenly everything went black. I must be dead.

DeFrantis spoke again, "I imagine it's all kinda confusing. I'm not sure who you are, or why you first attacked us, either. A lot of that can be sorted out later..."

"I attacked you?"

220

"Yeah, but..."

"Somehow it all went blank. I've been out of it for a while, haven't I?"

"Yeah, a few days, but, like I said, right now..."

"I attacked you? Why? What happened to me?"

Karendle interrupted, "Well, there were people on the barge fighting, then you jumped in, then I jumped in, then people got hurt, and you got trapped, and right now we just need to have you help us get unchained."

Eddiwarth took all this in. *I attacked? I got trapped?*

"We can sort all of that out some other time, though. We need to get out of here and find the children before anyone else comes back and tries to kill us. So, we'd really like for you to help." DeFrantis said, trying to smile in the dark. "Please?"

"So, I'm not dead?" This made Karendle laugh. *I guess not.*

I don't know. Sure. I can help, I guess. I don't know what's going on, but I guess I can help a couple of fair damsels in distress... He stood, then reached his hand out toward DeFrantis, and stopped, remembering. "Wait. How can I help if I can't use magic?"

DeFrantis sighed. "Yeah, that will make things difficult. But I think you can help us get our magic back." She shifted in place, shaking her chains, and pointed to the wall behind her. "Do you think you could break one of those windows?"

78

I Just Need a Little Air
DeFrantis

"What are you looking for?" DeFrantis asked, twisting painfully against the pillar she was leaning on.

Eddiwarth stood near the dark window, inspecting it. "I don't know. The glass looks pretty thick. It might be hard to break."

She wriggled some more and tried to use the tension on the chains around her wrist to straighten herself. "Come here."

Eddiwarth tapped on the pane. "Even if we break it, I'm not sure the opening would be large enough for us to get out." He looked back at DeFrantis. "Besides, we have to figure out how to get you out of your chains first."

Karendle added from across the room. "That's what we're trying to do. That's why we got you out."

DeFrantis added, "Come over here. I think this will help."

Eddiwarth stepped over to the pillar DeFrantis was chained to. "I'm not sure I understand what you're getting at." He grabbed the ring holding the wrist chains tight up above her head and tugged on them. "These feel pretty solid."

That's not what I'm talking about. Just focus on what I'm saying. She leaned forward, away from pillar, and arched her back. The position stretched her arms back behind her neck and she winced in pain. "Under my shirt, across my back, there's a small dagger. That will help you break the window."

"What?"

Just pay attention and focus! She sighed, then coughed. She leaned her head as far forward and down as she could. "Just reach down my collar, and find the small dagger that I hid there. It's not that hard."

"Reach down your shirt?"

Really? This is not that complicated! "Yes, and quickly. This hurts!". She hissed, "And don't think of grabbing anything but the dagger!"

He hesitated and slid his hand down her neck under her collar. His hands felt cold and the invasion was awkward. She felt his arm and hand inch closer to the steel that she had hidden there.

"Got it?"

"Yeah, I think so. It's not easy to grip." He slid his hand out slowly and pulled back. It was a small stiletto, more of roundel dagger. The blade was thin and triangular and came to a sharp point. It had a small metal handle, about as long as the blade, with a T-cross guard. The entire length was crusted with dried and smeared blood. DeFrantis flexed her back, shifting on the floor. *Ah! That's much better! That's been poking me ever since I hid it there.*

"Ok. Now take that, and use the blade to break the windows."

He still looked a bit confused, but he started walking over anyway. "Why do we want to break the windows?"

Oh, by the Creator, give me patience! "We need relief from the mage's bane smoke. If we can get some fresh air, maybe we can muster up the will to break out of these chains!"

"Just trust us and do it!" Karendle added. "But try to do it as quietly as possible...."

DeFrantis heard a few light taps as he nipped at the glass with the blade. Then there was a harder hit, and another one harder than that. A crackling and tinkling told her that he had done it. Immediately, she felt a slight and cool breeze dust across her legs. "Yes! That's it! Do another pane!"

There was another crack and the sound of glass on the floor. "How's that?" Eddiwarth called out.

Karendle said, "Now do one on the other end of the room, so the air blows through!"

As he moved, a bit of wind blew across DeFrantis' face, and she breathed deep, sucking in the cool air. She coughed as she got some of the dense smog in her lungs along with it. "I can... feel it! That's what we need!"

A moment later another crackle sounded and suddenly a more steady draft was coming into the room. As the smog grew thinner, DeFrantis breathed deep and felt that familiar surge as her head cleared and her will began to return. She could hear Karendle taking in air as well.

She brought her hands forward, focusing her attention and her will on the shackles. Her will was weak, but growing, as she surrounded the shackles in shadow. She pulled on them, tensing them against the pillar. She jerked and felt them cut into her wrists. *These chains that bind me will no longer hold me down. Now, I*

224

am their master! Now, they set me free!

She felt her arms and wrists relax and drop down into her lap as the shackles that held them dissolved into mists of shadow. She looked at them, and rubbed the soreness with her hands, her face in a smile of satisfaction. She hurried to her feet, and strode over to Karendle. "I'm out! Hold your hands up! Now it's your turn!" Karendle smiled and raised her shackles.

DeFrantis knelt next to her. As she started to focus on the chains, she heard the wind coming through the broken windows. The wind carried with it the sound of a child crying.

79
Scrybabies
Karendle

"That's right!" The tall man said, "You keep quiet and stop that crying!" Even hunched over, he towered over the small children huddled together on the pile of straw on the floor. His wrinkled and stubbly face was distorted into an angry scowl and his hair flopped down into his harsh and forceful eyes. The children cowered against the wall. Their shirts and faces were dirty, and the breeze through the window above them whisped their tangled hair.

The one that had been crying was trying hard not to burst out a second time. An older girl held him closer as he shook. She said, "We'll be quiet!" There were five of them, the oldest of which was the girl, with 10 winters at the most.

The man stood. "That's better. Now get to sleeping!" He backed away from them and returned to his chair. It was a wobbly wooden assembly, next to a slightly sturdier table. The table held a lantern, well-lit, a sword in a sheath, and a few half-drunk tankards of ale. On the other side of the table sat another man, not as tall or broad-shouldered. He had a full beard and and a rag tied tightly around his bald head. He grabbed some black and white knuckle bones off the table and rolled them between his hands.

"It's my turn, right?"

The taller man sighed, "I'm not gonna toss lots all night. I'm not giving you any more of my money!" He grabbed his tankard and drew a long swallow.

The other man ignored him and tossed the bones from his palms. They rattled across the tabletop and came to rest. "That's a three! The smaller man shouted. "I win again!"

Next to the straw that the children huddled on was another, smaller table, with a second lantern. It sat in the corner between two walls. In the second wall, next to the table, was a large, wooden door, with a latch and metal bands.

Karendle leaned up against the other side of that door, her eyes closed, her mind focused. Tightly clutched in both hands, directly before her face was a glowing blue stone. "I see two men, sitting at a table."

Eddiwarth stood directly behind her. He was not tall, but Karendle's half-dwarven stature made him hover over her. "Good, good..."

"This is working!" She whispered, excited, "It's working!"

"Yes, keep it down." He rested his hand on her shoulder. "Now, project your mind's eye further into the room. Turn it around. What else do you see?"

"Oh, by the Creator! I see them!"

DeFrantis stepped up behind them. "Who? Where are they?"

Eddiwarth shushed them.

Karendle whispered, "Four... No, five kids. They're huddled on a straw mat across from the men."

"Which ones? Who are they?"

"How should I know? Should I ask them their names?"

"Quiet!"

They all looked at each other for a moment. Finally, DeFrantis spoke. "You're right. Let's figure out how to take the men down." She took a breath.

"We only have the one dagger for a weapon, so we'll have to use our powers," Eddiwarth noted.

"Yes, but we don't know what we're up against, so lets be a bit cautious using our will. I can fill the room with shadow. That will give us a few moments of surprise." She looked at Eddiwarth. "If we need to, can you take down the door?" He nodded. "Karendle, you rush them. Maybe there'll be a sword you can grab"

"Alright, then." She held out her hand and focused her mind in the space beyond the door. She could feel the shadows swelling around her. They heard shouts from beyond the door.

"Let's go!"

80
Reunited, For the Moment
Eddiwarth

Eddiwarth steeled his shoulder and threw himself at the door. It banged loudly and he bounced off of it like coins tossed against a wall. "Ow! That hurt!" They heard muffled cursing and children's shrieks.

Karendle rolled her eyes. "Just blast it!"

Eddiwarth took a breath and pointed his hand at the door. With a loud crackle, bright lines of flashing electricity sparked between his fingers and the handle, shattering it into bits of metal and a thousand shards of wood. What remained spun inwards into the room. Instantly Karendle and DeFrantis ran into the darkness.

Eddiwarth could hear them as they stumbled, but the shroud of darkness hid everything. Karendle shouted, grunted, then he heard a crash. *That would be the table, I'd bet.* He heard a sword rapidly being drawn.

A man shouted, "What's going on? Where are you?"

What do I do? I can't see anything! He heard Kaendle's voice shouting, "I've got one! You're going down!"

Just as suddenly, the shroud of darkness dissipated into the shadows of the room, and Eddiwarth could suddenly see in the lanternlight. The table was upturned, and Karendle was struggling with one of the men. She was behind him, her arm around him in a choke hold. The other guard, the taller one, stood by the downed table, swinging his sword in confusion. Just as Eddiwarth was about to react, he saw something flash in DeFrantis' hand. *The dagger!* She ducked low, underneath the man's flailing arm, and lunged upward, plunging the blade deep into the man's chest. He gasped twice, then stumbled backward.

She hissed, "Stay away from my kids!" and pushed him down. He didn't get up.

Karendle pulled tighter on the man's neck as he thrashed on the floor, trying to dislodge her. He quickly succumbed to unconsciousness and Karendle shoved him aside. She looked up at Eddiwarth, "Thanks for the help!"

Eddiwarth was stunned and unsure what to say or do. The entire fight had just flashed past him like leaves blowing in the wind. The crying children brought his attention to focus again.

DeFrantis spun around and rushed to kneel with the children. "Andrina, Maresio!" She swooped her arms to embrace them, and they leapt into her arms. "DeFrantis! You've come!"

"It's OK. It's all going to be OK, now." She held them each and stroked their hair as they sobbed and climbed over her. "I'm here now. I'm here."

She leaned back and touched each one as she looked them over. "Where's Leyonne? And Toolie?"

The oldest girl shrugged. "We don't know. Someone took them away a few days ago!" DeFrantis dropped her head and reached around again to hold these five children close.

Eddiwarth and Karendle looked on at the scene before them. They glanced at each other, and that glance carried a loneliness, a sense of distance from their own parents.

230

A distant door slam and shouts shattered their reverie.

Eddiwarth ventured, "I thought this was a bit too easy."

81
A Fork in the Road
Thissraelle

Thissraelle had thought to rest in the back of the wagon as they traveled, hoping to restore a bit of her spent magical will, but the shaking and rocking of the wheels wouldn't let her. Finally, she gave up and sat, braced, against the side of the wagon bed, just trying to keep herself steady as she flipped and slid from side to side. She imagined the kids getting bounced around and felt bad for them. Suddenly with a jerk, the wagon stopped, and then rocked back a few inches. The creaking and rattling stopped, and all she could hear were the sounds of the forest birds and the horses nickering and stepping in place.

She crawled over the edge of the bed to look out between Antonerri and Granthurg. "What happened? Are we there?" She squinted out into the night, illuminated by the lanterns before the horses. She saw the road ahead split off into two directions.

"Which way?" She said

Granthurg shrugged. "I'm not sure. The horses seemed to know the way before, but now, they aren't moving ahead, either."

Antonerri asked, "Do we have that map?"

"No, it's back at the cathedral. They wouldn't let a book like that out of the house. Besides, the map wasn't that detailed. It didn't show every path or even every turn of this one."

One of the horses shook its harness, as if it were asking for direction. It stamped back and forth a little, but didn't pull to one side or the other. Antonerri stepped off the wagon and walked forward, unhitching one of the lanterns. He stood in the triangle of wheel ruts, inspecting them.

"None of them seem any more or less worn than any others." He took a few strides in one direction, trying to shine the light up the path a bit further. Then he came back and scouted up the other a ways, his lantern light disappearing behind the trees.

"Can you try to reach out to Karendle and see where they are?" Granthurg asked

"I can." She replied quietly. "Although I had been planning on saving my strength for the portal, or for the fight that follows."

Antonerri came back into view, shrugging. He reattached the light. The wagon shook a bit as he lifted himself up by the toeboard and climbed back onto the bench.

Thissraelle leaned back and found a place in the center of the wagon bed to sit. She closed her eyes and focused. She reached down inside of herself and felt her will surging. With a push, she sent it outward, forward, like a shock wave of soft blue rippling away before her. Her awareness stretched out between the trees, over the ridges, past the brush. Then she sat, waiting, motionless, as Antonerri and Granthurg looked on, wondering.

A few moments later, she felt a small surge return back to her. It wasn't forceful, but when it hit her, it snapped her eyes back open and her shoulders jerked. She pointed down the left fork.

"That way. It's not far, now!"

82

A Burning Wall of Fire
Karendle

They moved quickly down the darkened hallway. DeFrantis, determined, and surprisingly forceful, was in front. Behind her was Eddiwarth. Karendle was last, herding the five children in front of her.

DeFrantis called out from ahead, "I'm trying to find a doorway to get us out of the building quickly. Then, we'll be in a place to hide and possibly escape."

Karendle glanced down at the sword in her hand. She hefted it, feeling its balance. She had picked it up from the men they had just fought. DeFrantis had gotten the other one, and handed off the rondel dagger to Eddiwarth. *There's gonna be a fight. We don't have much, but we'll have to make do.*

Karendle was struggling to keep the kids moving. *They're scared, I get it. But we can't sit down and cry, here!* Her mind focused on the hallway and Eddiwarth's back to keep her own fear and tears down. *I just wanted to learn to be a mage. That's not too crazy to ask, is it? Just learn a few tricks? Now here I am chasing kids and running for my life!*

They rushed through an opening into a large hall. DeFrantis and Eddiwarth took in the space quickly, but Karendle couldn't see as well from the hallway's end. She could see some candelabras and tapestries on the far wall, and it looks like the ceiling was quite high. Maybe in its day, it was a grand ballroom.

"There's the door!" DeFrantis called out. Just as she started to move toward it, Karendle heard heavy footsteps and shouting burst into the room. She nervously shifted the sword from one hand to the other. She could see past Eddiwarth's shoulders into the room, where four or five armed men stood. It was dark, and she couldn't get a good look, but the threat was as heavy in the air as the mage's bane smoke had been.

The hushed moment when the two groups surprised each other was really only a matter of a second or two, but it seemed to suspend time. It broke when DeFrantis said, "Karendle, save the kids!", and the men rushed forward, swords drawn.

Karendle saw Eddiwarth crouch down low and sweep his hand in front of him. Halfway across the room, flames leapt up from the floor making a high infernal wall. Half of the men were surprised, and backed away from its heat, but others quickly started to turn around it. DeFrantis lunged forward.

Karendle backed the kids into the hallway and stepped between them and the opening to the room. *What to do? I can't just stand here and let the others get killed, but I have to guard the kids, too!*

Eddiwarth shifted forward and Karendle moved to the hallway opening to see what was happening. DeFrantis had engaged with one of the men. She was struggling to block his sword blows. Another stepped toward her, and Eddiwarth thrust his hand forward. The man was suddenly in the air, struggling to get footing, and flew backward into the wall. DeFrantis lost her footing on a rug and stumbled backward, then regained her balance. *She isn't doing well! She's probably saving her powers.*

Karendle turned back and looked at the frightened faces hiding in the shadows. *Maybe I can help from here, like Eddiword.* She dropped to her knees and set her sword down, then reached into her pouch and grabbed for the blue sapphire. Her hands shook as

234

she felt in the bag. She grabbed it and pulled it out, and another oculus fell out and clattered onto the floor. She ignored it, but gripped the blue gem in her hands. Karendle's gaze suddenly focused into the face of the oldest girl, who stood, hopeful, holding out the fallen stone. Her tiny voice bravely spoke, "Here. You dropped this."

Karendle reached out and took the dull grey stone from the girl. *Maybe... That might work!*

She looked up at the kids, who were all huddled together in fear. She smiled at them and said, "I have an idea, but I don't want you to be afraid. I'm not going to hurt you. Can you all be brave for me?" The oldest girl looked at the others, and then back up at Karendle as they all nodded. Their hopeful, dirty, and tear-streaked faces hit Karendle deep, like a punch to the gut.

"Alright, then!"

83
Stepping Through the Door
DeFrantis

DeFrantis' arm was getting tired as she struggled to block and dodge the relentless sword swipes of her attacker. She stepped backward from his press, trying to catch her breath and control her fear.

The swordsman swung in from the side and she leapt backward with a forward parry, barely glancing his blade away from her torso. As he swept his follow-through, she took the opportunity to reset her stance, regain her balance and ready her blade. She could see the doorway. On either side were windows showing the open night air. *If we can just get to them, we can be out!*

The heat from the fire and her own exertion was making her sweat, and she wiped her forehead with her free hand, gritting her teeth for the next strike.

The swordsman swung back, but DeFrantis misjudged the angle and his blade glanced off of hers and slashed into her shoulder. She shrieked in pain, and her own sword clattered to the floor. Her other hand clutched at her shoulder and felt the warmth of the blood as she stepped further back, away from escape. He smiled as drew back for a thrust.

An angry yell erupted from her left, and Karendle smashed into the man's side, toppling them both with a grunt to the floor. In the impact, he lost his grip on his own sword and it spun to DeFrantis' feet.

She looked on in amazement as Karendle shouted and began swinging fists at the man's surprised face. DeFrantis looked up. Eddiwarth was struggling to maintain the firewall, and it was beginning to catch onto the wooden floor, and the tapestries on the wall. She saw a man running around it, and rushing toward her.

DeFrantis crouched down, scooped up the sword, and brought it up in a sweeping block. *This one's much better balanced! I can swing this one!*

She stood and counterattacked, but the soldier easily stepped away. He pressed forward, with aggression and vigor. Even with the better sword, she was still on the defensive, and her shoulder weakened her.

"I can't hold this flame any longer!" Eddiwarth called out and collapsed to his knees.

236

DeFrantis couldn't respond. As she fought, she saw the man on the ground toss Karendle off of him and rise up over her.

"Just save the kids!" She shouted. *We'll do what we can.*

She coughed as she blocked. Smoke was starting to fill the room. Her attacker knocked her back and she stumbled down to one knee. She strained to stand again.

We'll do what we can.

To her right, a flash of silvery light appeared with a loud crackling noise, and both DeFrantis and the man stepped back to glance at it. A glowing ring grew in the open space of room, and she could see through it, like an opening into another place. *A portal? Oh, no! They're porting in more fighters! We have to run!* She struggled to move, but her legs were tired. *This is it. I can't move. We're done.*

Someone stepped through the widening ring. As he entered the room, she heard his familiar voice calling her name.

Antonerri!

He immediately rushed to DeFrantis, between her and the soldier. Antonerri swung his sword in an angry attack. Her attacker stepped back and blocked Antonerri's slash.

Antonerri!

She stood in the respite from the onslaught. She saw a larger, more imposing figure step through the gate, swinging a large warhammer.

Without Eddiwarth's focus, the firewall had subsided, even though the natural fires were still spreading across the floor. Three men stepped quickly through the flames and began running toward them.

She stood and reached out with her remaining will. Shadows swelled up from the floor and grew into tendrils tangling around their feet. One of them fell, struggling, but the others managed to step away and avoid the magic.

Granthurg plunged in, swinging his hammer.

DeFrantis felt hands on her shoulder, and winced. "You're hurt!" It was Thissraelle's voice.

We'll do what we can. DeFrantis gasped in exhaustion, then coughed.

84
Put the Hammer Down
Granthurg

Granthurg stepped through the portal, ducking low as it grew.

The room was large and well lit by flames dancing on the floor and running up the formerly elaborate tapestries on the wall. Right away, he saw his friends in trouble. To the right was Karendle trying desperately to fend off blows from a man grappling on top of her. To his left was DeFrantis, obviously exhausted. Antonerri had come through the portal first, and immediately engaged the soldier attacking DeFrantis. Their swords shimmered in motion with reflected firelight.

The heat from the fires was uncomfortable, as was the smoke they were creating. Granthurg turned the other direction, strode toward Karendle and, with a grunt, kicked the attacker off of her. The impact of a booted giant's foot rolled him away, coughing and gasping. The soldier stumbled to get up, just as Granthurg's upward swinging warhammer caught him straight in the gut. The impact lifted him and dropped him to the floor, unmoving.

Granthurg planted his stance and shouted, "Who's next?"

A taller, more muscular swordsman rushed at him, thrusting his blade. Granthurg stepped aside and turned the handle of his hammer to parry. The man was large, but not as massive as Granthurg, who braced himself low and used his leverage and hammer's mass to push the assailant back.

Granthurg saw a motion behind him, and glanced over his left shoulder to see. It was Karendle rushing over to support Antonerri. The swordsman before him used that second's hesitation to take another swing. Granthurg had to twist and step back to avoid it.

Granthurg caught the man's eye. He saw rage and aggression under his furrowed brow. *Is there a bit of fear there, too?*

The giant stepped back again, parried, and maintained the eye contact. His opponent's lips raised in a smirk. *Once more should do it...*

He used his giant legs to retreat back in a large stride. The swordsman lunged ahead, shouting, eager to take advantage. His confidence turned to surprise as Granthurg leaned back into his assault and swung his hammer in a low arc, sweeping the man's forward leg. Cracking, it fell out from under him, and he collapsed in pain on the floor. Granthurg lifted the Hammer around, up, and finally brought it crashing down onto the swordsman's chest.

Standing straight, he looked left to see the others. Antonerri had driven his opponent back to the fire on the floor, and Karendle was locking swords with another fighter. A thinner man, an elf, was behind the soldier, and Granthurg saw something small and silver flash in the elf's hand as he rushed forward, stabbing into her attacker's back. He stepped away and the man dropped his sword and collapsed.

Granthurg heard a voice shout from across the other side of the room. "This ends NOW!"

He saw two men enter the room from a hallway. They wore dark robes and cloaks. One of them immediately floated up over the flaming floor. The other crossed opposite him and stood ready, in a commanding stance. Granthurg recognized the dragon and flame icon stitched into the front of their robes. He smiled as he hefted his hammer and stepped toward the leader.

The other mage, from the air, extended his hand toward him. "Not so fast!" he shouted before pushing out a pulse of orange red power. It hit Granthurg square in the chest and exploded in a overwhelming flash of bright, noise, and pain.

When he opened his eyes, he was flat on the ground, several

yards from where he had stood before. His head hurt and his ears were ringing. He heard a distant woman's voice shouting, "Granthurg! Granthurg!"

Mom? Is that you, mom?

He looked at his hands and arms, now bloodied. Something was moving beneath him on his left side. He looked and saw a girl struggling to get out from under his back. *Who are you? What's happening?*

He felt hands on his other shoulder and turned his head. A pretty elf girl looked down on him with fear and worry in her face. "Granthurg! You're hurt!"

Thissraelle! I know you!

As Granthurg's awareness rushed back to him, and his head suddenly cleared, the pain in his arms and chest overwhelmed him as well. It hurt to breathe. It hurt to move. It hurt to be. He lifted his head and saw DeFrantis rush toward the mages with her sword drawn. The mage leader lifted his hand, dripping with blue light, and DeFrantis surged up into the air, kicking and choking.

I have to help her! Granthurg tried to move, to get up, to reach his hammer. His head spun before he fell back into blackness.

85
Into the Heart of the Stone
Karendle

The explosion ripped through the smoky air of the room, shaking the floor and bouncing back and forth between the walls. The

242

flash was harsh and blinding. Karendle was jolted off her feet, and fell. Something large and heavy fell on top of her, twisting her leg and pinning her to the floor.

She called out in pain, and tried to squirm free, but it held her pinned. She shook her head and tried to see. Quickly, her vision cleared, and she saw Granthurg's bloody shoulder over her hip. To her left was his warhammer, quietly resting on the ground. Just beyond that, the floor burned.

"Granthurg! Granthurg" She heard Thissraelle's frightened voice, and saw her run up to the other side of him. Her eyes reflected her fear and worry in the firelight. "Granthurg! You're hurt!"

Again, Karendle tried to squirm away, to turn her body, but the giant's weight was too much for her. With a bit of effort, she was finally able to shift so her hip hurt less. Thissraelle moved her hands over Granthurg, frantically trying to summon the the last of her will to heal him.

Beyond Thissraelle, she saw DeFrantis heft her sword, and rush forward. Karendle lay back and looked up to see the other mage floating above the fires. He was swirling his arms over the flames, using his striking powers to stoke them higher. She felt the heat growing, and saw him start to move the blaze forward toward her and Grathurg.

"Eddiwarll!" She called out, "Can you stop him?"

She heard no response.

"Eddiwarth!"

What can I do? Fear started her heart racing, making sweat bead

243

up on her face. *I can't move! We're going to die!*

Karendle reached to her chest to steady her heartbeat, and felt the pouch. She had hung it around her neck, thinking that it would be more secure than at her waist. She opened it quickly and and dug inside. *What can I do?*

She pulled out the stones. Two round and gray, one a sapphire gem. *He's a wizard, isn't he? Am I not supposed to catch wizards?* She smiled.

Wait, which one is it? This one? She held it up, studying it in the firelight. *Yeah. This one!*

She stretched out the stone toward the flying wizard, and focused deep. The intensity of the fear and the pain drove her will, and the silvery light came to the stone quickly. It shone brightly, even by the fire, and leapt forward to engulf the mage, pulling him down and out of the air. He struggled, shouting.

No! Karendle gritted her teeth, and squinted against flame's heat. *You're not hurting my friends any more!*

The mage's shape twisted, distorted, and swirled around the stone, until the light dissolved into it. Karendle dropped her exhausted arm.

"I got another one!"

86
The Light Shines
Antonerri

"DeFrantis!" Antonerri shouted, "Hold on!"

He shifted his sword and rushed toward the mage, who held her in a death grip in the air. Anger flowed through his arms. Rage drove his feet.

When he got only a few steps away, the wizard casually pointed and a blast of energy arced across the space between them. It hit Antonerri in the chest and shocked him, jolting him back from his trajectory. He rolled away, his legs twitching with the pain of the surge.

"You are all pathetic! What do you think you're doing? You ruin my market, attack my home, and kill my people..." The mage snarled, and stepped toward DeFrantis. She struggled, gasping for breath, her eyes widened with fear. "For what?"

He lowered DeFrantis until she was just a few feet off the ground and drew her forward to him. "For what? What is it you're trying to take from me? Street kids? Vermin? You should thank me for cleaning them out of the cities."

His gaze narrowed as his stare dug into DeFrantis' eyes. "They're nothing. NOTHING! Just to be meals for Dragons!" DeFrantis' eyes suddenly widened as the horror of the understanding struck her.

Don't touch her. Antonerri struggled against the pain in his limbs. He knelt, then stood. *I will save her. We will save them. You will not hurt them any more.*

The wizard broke his stare and raised his hand toward Antonerri again. "Stop!"

Antonerri stepped forward, and brought his sword up before him.

"You're determined, I can see," The mage said with tight lips. "Let me introduce you to PAIN!" More lightning surged from his outstretched palm, striking Antonerri. The energy shot through his limbs, driving him to his knees. Again and again, the mage blasted, tearing screams of anguish from Antonerri's throat.

Finally, he stopped, and Antonerri collapsed.

His body felt the pain, the familiar pain. *I took the blasts for you once before, and I lived.*

A new sensation rippled through his shoulders and down his spine, along with the pain. *I lived, and later, I chose to live.* He lifted himself up, and picked up his sword again, as the warm feeling

246

grew in him. *I choose to live, now. I will defend the weak. I will fight for the poor. I will fight for her!*

Antonerri stood and straightened his back.

The mage's blast struck again. Antonerri felt the jolt, felt the pain, but didn't scream. The warm glow strengthened with the blast.

I will fight for the children.

The wizard shouted in rage and tossed DeFrantis, gasping, to the side. He stepped toward Antonerri and threw shocking blasts at him with both hands. "You will die! Feel the Pain! Feel the Pain!"

Antonerri felt it coursing through his body. Pain wracked his limbs, but he stood. The light around him supported him, strengthened him, enlightened him.

The mage raged and blasted again, but it was much weaker. His will was fading. "Feel the Pain! Why don't you die?"

Antonerri coughed, then spoke. "Pain and I are old friends." He raised his sword. A familiar power welled up inside him, a light he had not felt in a long time. He focused this will into the blade. It burst into a bright radiance, with rays of light flowing off of it into the smoky air. He stepped forward, moving through the ache.

"You will not..." He stepped again. "You will not hurt anyone..."

The wizard took a step back, and fear rushed over him. He held his hands out before him, but no powers came.

"... EVER AGAIN!" Antonerri lunged forward in two deep strides and thrust his sword before him. He drove the bright

flaming blade deep into the mage's chest. The wizard gasped for breath, flailing his arms, grasping at Antonerri's shoulders. The sword's light burned through him. The wizard's eyes rolled up, his head dropped back, his legs failed, and he fell to the floor.

Antonerri turned around to see his companions staring at him. Granthurg sat up, and Karendle moved out from under him. Thissraelle stood, supporting Granthurg.

Antonerri looked down at his glowing sword and hands. As he straightened up, he saw DeFrantis where she lay on the floor. He rushed to her and held her head up. She was still drawing very heavy breaths, but her eyes were full of relief and tears. He slid his slowly dimming sword under his belt, and reached under her, lifting her up. He could feel her tension fade as the light absorbed into her. He called out to the others, "Gather everyone! Let's get out of here before it all burns down."

DeFrantis nodded and buried her head into Antonerri's shoulder. "Gather the children..." she mumbled with what breath she could muster.

87
Escape and Rest
DeFrantis

Antonerri grunted as he lifted DeFrantis up into the wagon. Then, he climbed up in to the bed and shifted her over. He covered her in blankets and she welcomed the warmth. As she settled, she reached up and took hold of Antonerri's arm. "Thank you," she breathed. He smiled, and moved to help the others as they approached the wagon.

She grabbed him and pulled him back. She said with a whisper,

"Where are the children? Are they safe?"

Antonerri's face suddenly flooded with awareness and surprise. "I.. I don't know..."

"Where are they?" She tried to sit up, "We have to find them! We're not leaving without them! I left them with Karendle!"

Antonerri gently set her back. He tried to remember. "Maybe she gathered them as we were escaping. Maybe Thissraelle has them." He tried to assure her, "I'll go see."

As he climbed out of the wagon, DeFrantis crawled to the back gate, looking out, but still too weak to get out. Karendle was approaching, limping, supported by Eddiwarth's only partly steady step. Behind them, with an equally labored pace, came Granthurg and Thissraelle. Granthurg's shirt was in bloody, tattered ruin, but his chest, arms, and torso were healed. Still, he was walking slowly and with stiffness.

"Where ar--" DeFrantis tried to shout, before lapsing into a fit of rasping and coughing.

"Where are the children?" Antonerri finished for her. "Did anyone see them? Did anyone get them?"

"Relax," Karendle said, "I have them. I kept them safe." She arrived at the wagon and leaned on it for support.

"Where are they?" Antonerri pressed, as DeFrantis gestured anxiously.

Karendle reached into her pouch and shook the oculi out into her hand. Two gray stones and one blue gem. She picked up one of

250

the gray oculi and held it up, with a self-satisfied smile. "I told the kids there was going to be a big, dangerous fight, and that I wanted to keep them safe. There was one place they could go where I knew no one could get to them! They were - I mean - are... very brave."

DeFrantis relaxed and nodded. She reached out and took the stone in her hand. She whispered the children's names as she cradled it close to her and settled back into the wagon. *We'll let them out when we're out of the forest. Out of danger.*

"Wait!" Karendle interjected, startling DeFrantis. She held up the other gray stone, then mumbled, half to herself, "Is this one the kids? Or is it the wizard?" She stepped forward and looked at them both very closely.

"That one's the kids." She pronounced, pointing. "I'm sure."

She looked at the one in her hand. "I think..."

Granthurg lifted Thissraelle up into the wagon bed, then moved toward the horses. Antonerri looked quizzically at Eddiwarth. "Who are you?" Eddiwarth's fine shirt was covered in dirt and soot, and he held up a grimy hand in greeting. He took a breath to speak.

Karendle interrupted, "He's with me." Antonerri glanced back at her. "Really, he's a good guy." Antonerri looked at DeFrantis, pointing both at Eddiwarth and Karendle. DeFrantis smiled and nodded. *Yeah, they're with me. They're with us.*

The old wagon creaked hard with the added weight of the extra riders, but it lurched ahead, tossing back and forth as it rolled away from the manor and into the forest.

251

88

The Light Shines Again
Antonerri

Antonerri picked up a short reed from the cup and gently held it in the flame of a candle. In a moment, it caught fire with a small tongue of its own flame. He brought it across the altar to light more candles. They were short and wide, each one in its own glass bowl. There were dozens of them, some fresh and stout, others burned hollow. The altar was long, with a soft velvet-covered kneeling stool running along it, all the way across the front of the chapel.

He lit twelve of them, then shook the reed, before it could burn his fingers. *Five for the ones we rescued at the manor, three for the ones we brought back from the market, and four for the ones we couldn't find.*

Several days of rest, herbal ointments, and care had done much to ease the pains he had endured. Still, he felt the soreness as he knelt before the altar and bowed his head. His mind reflected back on the changes these few short weeks had brought. His future was still uncertain. *I can't go back to the Holy Guard. In Twynne Rivers, I am a heretic, an outcast.* But, for now, the brothers here in the wooded abbey sheltered him and his friends, alongside the orphanage.

His mind flowed through thoughts of those he had fought next to. They were such strangers, but bonded together by circumstances. He felt the deep gratitude that comes with having good friends, a feeling he wasn't accustomed to. He heard a rustling of robes, and sensed someone kneeling beside him. He opened his eyes and looked, then smiled. "Brother Mathazar!"

"Forgive me for interrupting your prayers."

"Are you visiting the abbey?"

The friar shifted and sat on the altar stool. "When I heard that you had all returned with the children, I wanted to come see you!"

Antonerri smiled. "I'm glad you did."

Brother Mathazar smiled back. "That's a much brighter visage than what I saw before. You must be feeling much better." They embraced briefly. "You all placed your own lives in great danger for the lives of weak children. A few have returned to their parents, others are here in the orphanage. The slave market is in shambles. All of Dirae is talking about you."

Antonerri turned his gaze back to the candles. He looked deep into a flame. "I have seen light in other people where I thought it was gone." He remembered the feeling of warmth and brightness that had brought him out of the darkness in the manor house. "And I've seen the light inside of me again."

Brother Mathazar nodded. "I knew it was there."

Antonerri also nodded, and closed his eyes.

Light footsteps interrupted them, and they both looked back to see DeFrantis standing in the chapel aisle. The dress she wore was not as fancy or lacy as Thissraelle's style, but certainly finer than her rough and ragged street shirt and leggings. Her dark hair, though nicely brushed, still hung down into her eyes. They shone with a peace and calm that Antonerri had only come to see in the last few days. Standing behind her hip, behind her dress, was Lilia, a young girl of about 8 winters. Since they came back from the manor in the woods, she was never far from DeFrantis' side.

"The brothers in the kitchen have asked me to gather everyone for dinner..." She said, then waited for them. They stood and walked to her. She turned with them and they all stepped down the aisle together, with Lilia skipping ahead, her hair and dress swinging with each jump. The low afternoon sunlight shone through the tall stained glass windows, spreading heavenly vivid colors over the pews and onto the opposite wall.

"...And to remind you that we have scullery duty afterward."

The End of Story Two

Interlude

89
Stables and Stability
Granthurg

The smell of the warm summer night in the stables lingered with Granthurg as he crossed the courtyard to the main hall of the monastery. The cluster was surrounded by the trees of the Umbrawood Forest, keeping it well isolated from the rest of the world. Still, it wasn't too far from Dirae, and the cathedral there.

The lantern he carried shone brightly on the ground surrounding his feet. It was a traditional oil lamp, not a magical oculus gem, making the flickering glow. He stepped up onto the back patio of the abbey hall, and began to remove his large soiled boots. He knocked the dirt and muck off of them and set them by the back door, slipping some sandals onto his feet in their place.

In the two short weeks since they had returned from their battle to save the children, the monks of the abbey had been quick to figure out a way to make him sandals. Being a giant, about eight feet tall, his feet were easily twice the size of the largest human in the monastery, if not more. Making him a bed had been much more involved, so in the end, they gave him a thick pad of straw that they refreshed frequently. Being used to sleeping on the hard deck of his barge, he felt that to be the height of luxury.

After dinner this night, he had helped them get the draft animals in the stables, and put the carts away. It was often easier for him to just push the various carts and wagons into place, where it would often take two or three of the monks much more time to do the same work.

Now, as he entered the building, he turned down a hallway toward the great library. This was the time of the day he enjoyed the most. All was quiet, and he could relax by himself... *...and just learn! There are so many books and so many scrolls here! There is so much to for me to learn!*

With a click and a creak, he opened the great oaken doors and stepped into the room. He walked to the large table in the center and set the lantern down. He stepped over to one of the walls. They were covered, except where the windows stood, with shelves of books and racks of scrolls. Next to each window was a candelabra. Granturg carefully removed one of the candles and carried it back to the table to light it from the lantern's flame. Then, he began stepping around the room, lighting each of the candles mounted by each window.

He was about half-way around when he stopped. In one corner of the room there were some large and comfortable chairs. Thissraelle was sitting there, waiting for him.

Granthurg smiled. Her small high-elven frame seemed to be

almost swallowed up in the huge seat. Her whispy, light hair and white tunic contrasted sharply against the deep red-brown leather. She smiled, too, but less enthusiastically.

Oh-oh. Something's bothering her. I can tell.

He carried on lighting the candles. "It's been a beautiful summer's day, hasn't it?"

"Yes, beautiful."

Granthurg laughed. "I wasn't serious."

She tossed her head back onto the chair and let out a long sigh. "You know me too well."

Yes, I know you pretty well. He'd only known her about a month. But in that time, they'd travelled and faced dangers together, and shared many secrets. They had become very close friends. "Let me guess: Karendle's not getting it."

"No! Not at all!" Thissraelle blurted out. "She doesn't have a magical bone in her body! There! I said it! She wants it so bad, and she tries so hard, but she just can't do it!"

"No matter how you show her...?"

"I've tried so many different ways to explain it. I've tried to teach her so many things." She wiped her eyes with her hands in a vain attempt to find some clarity, or at least to ease away the tiredness. "Nothing I try works. She gets so tense!"

"What about those flying stones I had to dodge the other day?" He asked, "That seemed to be working."

"Yes, but that was using the oculus. As long as she's using the gems, she can use magic. It's like she has no will of her own. And Eddiwarth! I shouldn't even start talking about him!"

Granthurg sat down next to her. "He's not helping?"

"No! Definitely not helping. He jumps in and starts using his own powers to mess with her. He thinks he's helping, but he just frustrates her more. Today, they got in a big argument. I just left them out in the forest."

"Maybe you could just turn them both into rocks that they could toss at each other." The look that she gave him showed that she did not at all think that was funny. "...Or not."

"I'm not helping them. I don't know why I'm trying, really."

There's more to this. I can tell. He turned in the chair to face her and looked with a skeptical eye.

"I'm serious! Really! Why am I helping them?" She put her head in her hands, then looked up at Granthurg. Her voice got quiet. "You were there. You heard them tell their stories. They were both after me, trying to capture me. Karendle would have sold me off, and Eddiwarth was going to fetch me back to my father. So, why am I helping them?"

I want to tell her that it's all going to be fine. That they're a part of the team, and they've changed. But I don't know that for sure, either. He put a hand on her shoulder. It looked awkward, as large as it was, but it seemed to soothe Thissraelle. She leaned into it. "I think you're the only one I can fully trust, here."

"You're helping them because you have a large, kind heart.

Really, you're the heart of the team. It's true that without any of us, we wouldn't have been able to rescue the kids. But without you drawing us all together, it wouldn't have happened in the first place. DeFrantis and Antonerri would have tried on their own." He let out his own sigh. "And you know how that would have ended."

"Yes. I guess." She nodded and leaned up against him. "...But is it safe for me here?"

"It may not be."

I wish it were, but it might not be.

90
Dance the Circle
Antonerri

"DANCE THE CIRCLE!" The jester called out, "EVERYONE! JOIN IN! YOUNG AND OLD!" The bells dangling from the points on his hood jangled as he spun. His shirt was a loose pattern of colored triangles, and his baggy pants flapped with the motion of his prancing legs.

It was a hot, sunny, and muggy day. It was the time of the SummerFaire, three days of celebration. Dirae was not a large city, but neither was it a tiny village. It was an important trading spot between the palaces, shops, and slums of the City of Twynne Rivers, and the western hamlets along the Wynne River. The faire brought in celebrants from many miles, drawn to the festivities by the diversion from their labors as well as the chance to buy and sell.

The streets along the city plaza, not too far from the waterfront, were lined with tents, and full of people. There were more children out now, as parents felt safer in the town. Colorful streamers were strung from tree to building and building to tree. The smells of roasting nuts and newly-baked breads blew through the plaza with the breezes.

"WHO'LL JOIN ME?" The jester called out, continuing his swirls. He stopped, smiled across the crowd that had gathered, and slowly looked around. From his left, a drummer sitting on the ground began to slap out an energetic beat and, in a moment, a fiddler and a piper jumped into a melody.

"YOU WILL, WON'T YOU?" He pointed at DeFrantis. She barely had a moment to object before he had leapt over to her and taken her hand, dragging her forward. She laughed and shrieked, then reached out to grab the hand of Lilia, the young girl standing next to her. The girl, and two others, skipped into the circle, shouting and laughing.

Granthurg called out to them, as Thissraelle and Eddiwarth began clapping along with the music. Antonerri watched them go with a thin smile on his own face, wanting to jump in, but holding back, a little bit timid. They fell into the rhythm of the music and the many people in the plaza stepped aside to make room for the circle. Others grabbed hands and joined the line as it passed them. More children got in the line, along with their parents.

Antonerri couldn't help but stare at DeFrantis as she danced, hand-in-hand with the jester and the kids. Her dark hair also danced as she looked back and forth from the jester to the children. She had tried to braid her dark hair that morning before they left, but it just wasn't long enough yet. She had been quite a bit frustrated in trying, but in the end had settled for a simple

260

cloth and bead headband. When they had arrived at the plaza, some of the girls had handed her some flowers they had picked and those were now twisted into that band and her hair. Those flowers now bounced with her locks against her forehead and down over her laughing eyes. The tune was familiar, and she and most of the dancers began singing along.

As the chain of dancers circled around to the music for the third time, the Jester reached out and grabbed Antonerri's arm, giving him a shove into the line. Jerked out of his trance, Antonerri shouted and stumbled his way along.

The musicians picked up the pace, making it even harder for him to keep his proper footing. After a few moments, he gave up trying to match the steps and just jumped along in the line. In the confusion, he glanced over and saw DeFrantis laughing at his fumbling feet.

The music changed up again, and the jester stepped aside and closed the gap by bringing the two hands he was holding together. He spun away into the center, shouting, "DANCE THE CIRCLE! CIRCLE ROUND AND ROUND!" Antonerri suddenly realized the hand he was now holding was DeFrantis'. Instantly, he caught his breath, his mind went blank, and he almost lost his balance. A few quick side steps and he was back on his feet, jumping along.

"Try and keep up, old man!" He heard her say, and her voice mixed with the melody and the singing. He had to look down at his feet and catch his balance. He happened to look up and matched the jester's eyes. They had a knowing smile that seemed to say, "You're welcome!"

"Hey-o, hey-o..." DeFrantis' sang with the crowd. He smiled at her, but didn't know the melody. He didn't have the breath to sing, anyway. "Hey-o, Hey-o," The kids sang with her, as the musicians brought the tune and the dance to an end. The children began cheering, and everyone dropped their hands, clapping and laughing.

Except Antonerri. He just stared and smiled at her, and she at him. He didn't let go. He gently tugged her closer.

91
A Sunny Day
Antonerri

"Your beard has come back in very nicely," DeFrantis said, running her fingers across his chin. They relaxed under a tree in a field not too far from the faire. The sun was high in the mid-afternoon, warming the grounds and the air. Somewhere the clack of wooden swords and the shouts and music of the celebration rang out, but the two were oblivious. She was half sitting, half lying on the grass as he rested his head in her lap, on the folds of her linen dress.

"I'm keeping it trimmed, but...," he paused for a breath, "But the last time I actually shaved was over a month ago."

He went quiet for a moment, as he thought back on all that happened that morning. *A lot has happened since then. A lot has changed. She's not so timid any more, not so likely to hide her beauty in the shadows. She's brought me into light as well.*

"I remember that day," she chuckled, "You tried to sell me into slavery!"

"You told me to! It was your idea!"

262

He listened to her musical laugh. He also remembered that day. He remembered the fear. *I remember the explosion, and the fight. Trying to find you, and find the children. That was a very dark day for me. I was so lost, so confused. Then at the cathedral...*

Her voice got quiet, "There were many times, when we were in the manor, in chains, and then later, in the fight... Many times that I as good as gave up. I felt so alone. I didn't know if you would ever find me. But I had to get out. I had to save the children. I gave all I could in the fight, but it wasn't enough. I thought we were done. I thought it was over."

A breeze blew across them, bringing a bit of cool in the warm shade. He started to speak, but she shushed him with a finger on his lips. "And then you stepped through Thissraelle's portal and I heard you call my name."

She breathed deep and looked down on him, "That was all I needed. I heard you call my name, and it was like I could breathe again. Somehow you had found me, and that was all that mattered. I knew we would do it. I didn't know how, but I knew we could win."

She continued, "And then I saw him hurting you, and I knew how much that pained you. I remembered from the dungeon. I wanted to take the shocks like you had done for me. And then I saw you alight with power..."

Antonerri sat up and faced her. He reached his arm around her. "It was your determination that saved the kids. I had to find you. It was you that saved me."

He kissed her once, then again, then held her, face-to-face.

She reached up, embraced him, and held him, close and tight, not letting go.

In the distance, music played on, and people danced in the summer sun.

92
Winds of Change
Karendle

The Inn was noisy, crowded, and a little dim, in spite of the candles on the walls and the tables. Night had fallen on the last day of the SummerFaire, and so before going back to the monastery in the woods, the team sat down for a grand meal. The air was filled with the smattering of conversations mixed with the smell of stews, breads, and roasts. Many others who were there for the faire had also gathered to eat or to stay a night before leaving town to return home.

Karendle sat with her companions around a long, oval table. She picked up her ale and took a swig, while listening to the conversations.

"Where's the food?" Granthurg complained, "I'm hungry"

"You're always hungry," Thisraelle chirped.

I can't quite figure them out. They seem almost inseparable, but yet they don't quite fit together. I don't think Thissraelle likes me much. I'm not sure why. It's nice that she's trying to teach me magic, but she's not very patient with me. Maybe that's the problem.

"At least we have plenty of ale!" Eddiwarth drew deep on his tankard.

264

I do wish he would leave me alone. I think I would learn a lot faster without him interfering. He's just fixated on Thissraelle. Maybe Granthurg will finally get fed up and take him out behind the stables someday. He could sure use a good thrashing.

Antonerri just laughed. He sat near DeFrantis, with his arm across her chair, around her shoulders. She was leaned in close to him.

Karendle took another drink. The inkeeper's wife stepped up to the table, and said, "Here we are! Thanks for waiting!" She started putting bowls on the table. "Stew! Bread! And lots of seasoned apples!" Everyone leaned in and picked up bowls and plates, passing them around the table.

"Oh, this is great!"

"Careful, it's hot"

"Here's the bread"

Karendle took in the scene as the aromas drifted up from her bowl. She glanced up at DeFrantis. *I owe her my life. I owe her everything. I still don't understand why she helps me. Maybe she just helps everyone.*

DeFrantis held up her hands and spoke, "Hello, before everyone starts eating--"

"Too late!" Thissraelle said, laughing at Granthurg.

DeFrantis smiled, and Granthurg awkwardly set his bowl down. She continued, "This last month has changed my life. Everyone seems to look at me when we talk about our adventures, but we all brought the children home. We all fought together. Now, for the first time, I truly have a home." She smiled at Antonerri, who gave her shoulder a squeeze. She stood and lifted her tankard. "Thank you all. Each of you risked your life for mine, and for the sake of the kids. Thank you, my dear friends!"

Everyone drank and cheered as she sat back down. Karendle nodded before drinking. *I have never felt this before. I have never felt this... closeness... this belonging.*

She took a bit of bread, dipped it in her stew and began eating. *What am I to do, now? I can't return to Twynne Rivers. I'm not sure how long the monastery will let me stay there.*

Her thoughts were interrupted by the cry of "Hear, ye! Hear, ye!" Everyone turned toward the main door to see the source of the interruption. It was the pubcrier, there to call out the week's news. As he started, people in the inn returned to their dinners. Karendle quickly tuned him out as well, until she heard him mention the Twynne Rivers Wizard's Guild. She and Thissraelle both snapped up their attention and turned around to listen.

"...The Wizard's guild has long opposed any attempt by the Royal Court to impose laws limiting the use of magic. However, King Hastone III, of House Twynham, may he live long, and protect us all, has issued a decree of a tax of 5 coppers to be levied against anyone using magic powers in a public place. Anyone using such powers and refusing to pay the toll will be arrested. His majesty decrees this as necessary to regulate the wanton chaos brought about by uncontrolled wizardry!"

The pubcrier continued on, "SummerFaire celebrations will continue throughout this month in various towns and hamlets throughout the Realm. Those travelling the roads will be subject

266

to th..." The attention the group paid to the pubcrier faded as they all turned back to the table to look at each other with questions on their faces. Bits of conversation drifted from other tables, "It's about time they did something to stop them!", "They should lock all the wizards away, I say!"...

Thissraelle seemed particularly disturbed. Eddiwarth asked, "So, what does this mean? What's happening?"

"My father would never allow this!" Thissraelle crossed her arms, her head down. "Never!"

Karendle felt a chilly draft blow across the table, and shivered.

There's more of the story, with these and more characters at TheHerosTale.com.

What's the dragon up to? Why is everyone hating on the wizards? What's going on in the Church of Three Lights?

Come find out...

Acknowledgements

Many thanks to all those who helped in life and in this project in particular: Jodi Hansen, Brendon Hansen, Jacob Hansen, Tyler Luckau, Doug Bedwell, Jaclyn Weist, Jared Quon, Sasha Justine, Avery Myrup, Avery Kirk, Jared Carnes, Jessica Carnes, Ruth Hollander, and many others!

About The Hero's Tale

The Hero's Tale is a Fantasy Role-playing Game published by The author and his sons. It's an attempt to show how to use tabletop RPGs to strengthen family bonds and to teach life lessons in a more fluid and story-driven system.

In the core rule book, there is a beginning adventure module, entitled, "The Haunted Abbey of Haffenberg". The story you've just read uses the pre-made characters available for this adventure, and the world the adventure is set in.

To learn more, visit TheHerosTale.com

About the Author

Mark Hansen has been writing and studying writing for most of his adult life. Though "A Tale of Heroes" is his first published work of fiction, he has written many books and blogs over the years. He currently lives in Eagle Mountain, UT, and loves to play geeky games with his sons.

Other books and games by Mark Hansen

- The Hero's Tale – How to Use Tabletop RPGs to Help Raise Great Kids – TheHerosTale.com
- Seeker's Quest – A collectible card game based on the scriptures of the Church of Jesus Christ of Latter-Day Saints – SeekersQuestGame.com
- Best of the Black Pot, Around the World in a Dutch Oven, Dutch Oven Breads, 4 others – Dutch Oven Outdoor Cookbooks – MarksBlackPot.com

Mark's Social Media

- Twitter
  - @theherostaletht – The Hero's Tale
  - @mrkhmusic – MormonGamer
- Facebook
  - facebook.com/groups/theherostale